ROCKHAND
LIZZIE

Gerald Eugene Nathan Stone

GStone 6-99

HAPPY BIRTHDAY 7-6-99
NOW YOUR LIBRARY HAS
TWO BOOKS.

TATTERSALL
PUBLISHING

Tattersall Publishing
P.O. Box 308194
Denton, Texas 76203-8194
www.tattersallpub.com

First Edition

Printed in the United States of America

02 01 00 99 010 1 2 3 4 5

Cover Illustration by Patrick Kirl
Text Ornaments by Gerald Eugene Nathan Stone

Library of Congress Catalog Card Number: 99-70932
ISBN 0-9640513-6-2

Stone, Gerald Eugene Nathan. Rockhand Lizzie /
by Gerald Eugene Nathan Stone.
179 p.
Summary: Following the death of her parents and the break-
up of her family, young Lizzie Tackett relies on her wits and
her amazing accuracy in throwing rocks and washers to survive
in rural Arkansas in the early 1900s.
ISBN 0-9640513-6-2
[1. Orphans - Fiction. 2. Arkansas - Fiction]
I. Title. 1999 [Fic]

ACKNOWLEDGEMENTS

My own Mother's journey as an orphan is the nail on which I hang this story, but the story itself is my own tattered embroidery.

My editor, Crystal Wood, has once again worked to repair the tears in the cloth, and hopefully she has restored the pattern for your view.

To my Mother,
Julia Elizabeth Marshall

THE WINTER WIND IS WHISTLING AROUND THE DOOR AND RATTLING THE windows. When one of these blue northers comes blasting over the Kansas border, it follows the Canadian River like a funnel and settles the full weight of its coldness here in these Oklahoma bottomlands. I can see out the window the cuptowels I hung on the clothesline this morning standing straight out like little white flags, stiff-frozen in the wind. I reckon they can wait; they ain't worth my going out there now and breaking a hip.

It's plenty snug here in the house. Mark built it good and tight to keep it that way, but I can still hear that bitter wind. When it blows like this, a chill of memories from years ago comes in like a flood, bearing before it like flotsam the painful scenes of my childhood. Oklahoma warn't even a state then—it was still the Indian Territory, not just in name but in the faces of the solid, silent natives who watched us Boomers flocking in from the east. Arkansas warn't that far to the east, but it was a whole lifetime away...

GERALD EUGENE NATHAN STONE

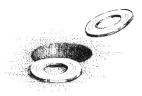

CHAPTER ONE

THEY SAY YOU CAN'T REMEMBER YOUR EARLIEST YEARS, BUT I CAN. Ours was a sharecropper family, and our home a typical Arkansas dogtrot. Go up the front steps onto a long front porch, or continue straight ahead down the dogtrot. On one side was the kitchen, and on the other, lined up in shotgun fashion, was the parlor, then two bedrooms. We ate in the kitchen in the winter and in the parlor in the summer, because of the heat from the cookstove. Not only was the kitchen the warmest room, it was also the most dangerous. My bachelor uncle Elliot had slept through a rainstorm one night and when he stepped onto his dogtrot to go to the kitchen to fix breakfast, the kitchen was gone—it had burned down during the night.

We started taking all our meals in the kitchen, and moved Ma's bed into the parlor the spring that Pa had his accident. He had been trying to help a neighbor get his turning plow loose from a new ground stump, when a hitched mule up and kicked him in the small of the back. They brought him home in a wagon, and helped us put him in the bed in the parlor so he could be close to the kitchen and share in the mealtimes. But that mule must have kicked the spirit out of Pa; he never got out of the bed after that, eating less and less, and wasted away within the month.

After Pa died, Ma worked in the fields like a woman possessed. She worked like she had to hoe the whole field before dark, and the faster she hoed, the shorter grip she took on the hoe handle. By the time she got to the end of the row, she was bent almost double, and was gripping the hoe down near the head. Her only reprieve was to raise up occasionally to get a breath and say, "Lawd-a-mercy, we've got to hurry!" Of course, we kids tried to keep up with her out of shame, but I couldn't help but wish that we could at least work like those sharecroppers on Mister Cunningham's place. Most of them were darkies, and they didn't have it any better than we did, but at least they took time to sing. I remember hiding in the grass along the edge of the field one time, listening to their songs, watching their rhythmic march down the rows, dressed to the hilt in black overcoats and hats, or black dresses and bonnets, standing upright, swinging their hoes in time with each other, getting so much done with so little effort.

But Ma finally played out after cotton picking was over, and took to her lonely bed. How cold it was in that record-breaking Arkansas winter of 1901, when I was going on seven. My three older brothers, gangly William, seventeen, silent Patrick, eleven, and fun-loving Jake, nine, were huddled over in the corner of the parlor, staring out the window into the dying light.

My older sister, Josie, who was eight, was gripping the foot of the rusty iron bedstead till her knuckles shone like peeled grapes, determined not to cry. The only sounds were the ticking of the clock over the mantel, an occasional pop from some dying ember in the fireplace, the rise and fall of the wind like an expiring giant, and our hounds bumping around under the floor, hiding from the cold and giving an occasional mournful howl. I had just lit the oil lamp and set it on the bedside table, and was looking at Ma. She warn't going to do no more hoeing. But there was no peace to be seen in her face, just an empty tiredness. How thin she was, with her high cheek bones that she said came from her Indian forbears stretching her sallow skin, her china blue eyes from some Scottish bloodline sunken and sightless. How pathetic she looked under that old ragged quilt. She had died, weak with consumption, but furious at the

4

thought of leaving her younguns.

William had gone down the road after Miz Robbins earlier that bleak afternoon, but Ma was gone long before they got back. Died and gone in the same room and bed where Pa died. It was the emptiest room in the world. Thinking on that I fell across the bed, and tried to bury my grief in that old quilt.

When Miz Robbins got there I had to be pulled off of Ma's body. Miz Robbins closed Ma's eyes with some coins she had in a knotted sock in her apron, and covered her face with the quilt. I couldn't stand the sight of that quilt pulled up over Ma's face, and plucked it off. I realize now that she did it out of kindness, but at that moment I hated Miz Robbins, and jerked the quilt back down where I could see Ma. Miz Robbins and I fought in a repetition of that hopeless routine, until I wearied and sank into a bitter keening, "Ma, please speak to me!"

"Hush now, Lizzie, honey," Miz Robbins said gently, "Your ma's gone to heaven to be with your pa. She'd want you to be a brave little girl right now." That didn't make me feel any better, but by then I was too tired to argue. Miz Robbins sent me and Josie across the dogtrot to sleep in the kitchen that night so we could stay a little warm, and our brothers to the back bedroom, saying she would stay and watch up with Ma till morning light.

Come morning my brothers dug the grave next to Pa's, on a small hill crowned with some cedars about a stone's throw from the front porch. Jim, a darky who lived behind Mister Cunningham's house at Perry, was there to help, but after the grave was finished he stepped over to the grove of cedars, and watched our grief from a distance. After country custom we took care of our own when there was a death. Josie and me had washed Ma and laid her out in her feed sack dress, and then wrapped her in the Wedding Ring quilt she had brought from Tennessee. We didn't expect anyone but Miz Robbins to come for the burying, but the Perry storekeeper, Mister Cunningham, showed up with Isaac Haskins, who was a business partner of his and fellow Lodge member. They watched while the clods fell on the Wedding Ring quilt, and as the grave was filled in. Josie and me patted the dirt down smooth with our bare hands in that cold wind.

I looked up and saw Haskins and Mister Cunningham walk around the house, then they eyed us several times, saying nothing, and went down to look at the barn. Haskins didn't even pull off his black hat. Patrick, my quiet brother, was grieving down near the corn crib, and I guess he heard them talking. I seen him stalking to the house, stiff and furious. He passed us, went into the kitchen, then came out carrying a spit can and crossed the dogtrot to Ma's bedroom. Then he came out muttering, "They ain't a-gonna have it." I watched him going around the corner of the house and then smelled coal oil at about the same time that flames started licking out the door and window openings of first the kitchen, and then the bedroom.

Jake broke for the door crying, "No! No!", and I tried to follow him. But William grabbed me by my pigtails as I ran by him, tripped Jake, and we all fell down. William pinned us both down long enough that when we got loose it was too late to try to get in the house. Haskins and Cunningham came running up, confused and angry. They didn't see Patrick circling the house and heading for the barn. Haskins and Cunningham halfheartedly threw some buckets of water from the rain barrel on the flames, but couldn't get close enough to do any good. Haskins threw the bucket into the flames in disgust, then whirled around at a "whooshing" sound from the barn. Patrick had set it too, and flames were leaping into the sky as animals scattered in every direction. Haskins roared in helpless rage, and raced off to the plum thicket behind the barn, thinking he would catch Patrick there.

Yes, I remember when I was going on seven. I also remember the cold rage that Haskins and Cunningham leveled at us when a crony judge of theirs parceled out us kids to the four winds. William was sent to the Mayberrys, but he didn't stay long—he left with his sweetheart for the Indian Territory within the month. They sent Jake to Atkins, across the river, and set him to work there in a barrel stave yard. Patrick, my silent incendiary, they never caught. He left for the Indian Territory too, but not before he burned Haskins' farmhouse down. That left Josie and me, to be pried apart by Mister Cunningham. He took Josie away, and I was left with Miz Robbins for the time being.

GERALD EUGENE NATHAN STONE

CHAPTER TWO

L IVING WITH MIZ ROBBINS WAS A STUDY. SHE STAYED UP AT NIGHT A LOT, sitting by the window in the dark, rocking occasionally, but mostly just sitting and looking out the window. Actually I never saw her sleeping or even in a nightgown. I studied about that a lot.

She warn't a widow—her husband had been committed to the insane asylum in Little Rock just before Pa died. I remember when it happened. Josie and I woke up at the same time one night, hearing these muffled shouts coming from down the road. It was Mister Robbins shouting from his storm cellar where Miz Robbins had locked him in. Josie and I got up and crept outside, listened without satisfying our curiosity, then beat it down the lane to where we could see what was going on. The night air was vibrating with Mister Robbins' drunken yelling in the cellar, and like a shadow in the moonlight stood Miz Robbins beside the cellar door with an upraised shovel. We sensed that William had come up behind us. He slapped our behinds and said to git on back to our bed—he was going get the constable. Josie and me dawdled until he left, then settled down again in the shadows to see what would happen.

We listened to what sounded a lot like a camp meeting. Mister Robbins would sing about being washed in the blood, then he would break out in hellfire and damnation, then he would wheedle Miz Robbins to open the door. She didn't waver. Finally the constable got there on his mule with William riding behind, and a couple of other men on mules, carrying a wagon sheet and some bed slats. The constable had his shotgun and some shackles. He took a stance in front of the door, and told Miz Robbins to open the door and stand back. Out of the darkness within came "Lo, and the grave shall give forth her dead," and Mister Robbins came into view, climbing the dirt steps, staggering a little bit, buck naked, covered with sweat, still carrying a liquor jug in the crook of one finger. As he stepped into the full moonlight, we could see that his feet were bloody from tromping who knows how many fruit jars during his night ragings. He was a tall gaunt man—not much of a farmer, according to Pa, and given to itinerant preaching in the hills around Yell County—but he still had plenty of energy.

He surveyed his congregation, made a move toward his wife, and a melee began. After they got him rassled down, they trussed him up in the wagon sheet, with the slats to keep him from kicking, and put him in his own wagon. After hitching up two of the mules, they headed off towards Hollis, which Josie and I took as our signal to skedaddle back to bed. As we left we could hear some vaguely familiar Old Testament passages being laid on everybody in sight, especially on Miz Robbins. There were so many "Woe!"s in his ranting, that if it had been daylight, every mule within two miles would've stopped dead in its tracks.

About six weeks after I went to live with Miz Robbins, she took me with her to the store at Perry, and found that they had a letter waiting for her at the Post Office in the back corner of the store. I was lolling around the candy case, watching the flies crawling around on the inside of the glass, wondering why, when they had finally got to where they wanted to go, they were trying to get out. I remember her turning that envelope over and over before opening it with a trembling hand. She asked Miz Cunningham's sister, Miz Sally, who worked in the store and ran the Post Office, to read it to her. Well, the news was from Little Rock saying that Mister Robbins had broke out of the asylum, and they couldn't find him.

Now I could ordinarily keep up with anyone, having follered Pa in the furrows ever since I could remember, but I had trouble keeping up with Miz Robbins going home that day. She was in some hurry! Life changed. Miz Robbins became as nervous as a cat. She spent the days watching the road coming in from the barn and the lane at the front of the house. Then she spent the nights watching and waiting at her bedroom window. Just waiting. I didn't understand exactly where Little Rock was, or even in what direction, but after watching Miz Robbins spend the rest of that winter watching through that window, I knew he would be back one day. It got to where I would start at every shadow, day or night. To my mind it didn't help matters any to remember that Mister Robbins and Haskins had been thick as thieves.

Feeling blue one day during the following spring, I decided to go down to Perry to see Josie. I counted on Haskins being busy in the bottoms, breaking up new ground, and lining up his sharecroppers, so there warn't any danger of running into him. That left Cunningham, and he was surely downstairs minding his store. Since Josie had a room up over the store, I went around to the back and chunked some pebbles at the upstairs window, thinking Josie would hear me and come outside to talk. Almost before the pebbles had bounced off the window and hit the ground, the window flew up so fast, a couple of its lights fell out. And there, sticking his head out the window, was old Haskins. He saw me, and hollered, "Where is that hussy sister of yourn? You brats have got something cooked up, haven't you? You just hold still, I'm a-coming down."

It seemed like every time I turned around I was running into Haskins. I didn't know what he was doing at the Cunningham's store, much less in Josie's bedroom, but I didn't stop to try and figure it out. If Josie warn't there, then I didn't intend to be neither, so I lit out. Straight back to Miz Robbins, like a transgressor flying for the City of Refuge.

When I got there, I went around to the back and leaned against the wall, out of breath and fanning my skirt. If Miz Robbins didn't know I was home, and Haskins came looking for me, she wouldn't have to lie about where I was at.

I had a stitch in my side, so I spit, and bent down to put a rock on top of the spittle. It worked, like always. Straightening up, I noticed that things were mighty quiet and still. After a time I decided maybe Haskins had decided not to foller me after all, so I snuck in the house. Hearing nothing, but still jumpy, I crept towards the front of the house where Miz Robbins spent most of her time.

Miz Robbins was there, all right, sitting in her chair in front of the window, but she warn't rocking. I stopped in the doorway and sorta cleared my throat, saying, "Ma'am, that Haskins is after me agin!" When she didn't answer, I entered the room and came up behind Miz Robbins and saw part of a broken fruit jar on the floor behind the rocker. Staring at it, I came around the side of her chair to the horror of seeing my last friend in the world with the bottom half of a fruit jar jammed into her throat. Then I saw the blood, everywhere the blood, and padding through it were the bare footprints of a grown man. For the second time in less than an hour I lit out.

All that day I walked the woods, and into the night. After the moon came up, I could see some familiar trails leading through the berry patches, so I warn't lost. I made my way on down the trail to a hillside cemetery, one I remembered from picking huckleberries there last summer. I needed to find a place to rest, but I didn't care anything about sleeping among the chiggers and ticks, or over a snake hole, so I looked for the freshest grave I could find, thinking it would be free of varmints. I found one in the dappled moonlight and out of sight of the path, and tumbled down, bone weary and not caring much any more.

The moon was still high when I woke up with a start. I warn't worried about sleeping on a grave—what I was worried about was something alive and somewheres behind me. I figured if Haskins, or Mister Cunningham, or Mister Robbins, or all of them, was out looking for me, that they would shy away from the cemetery, or at least figure that I would. When you're scared, you get a conniving mind. Still, I didn't relish being anywheres in the country near them.

Things were quiet again, which is unnatural in the woods, so I rose to light out again. Some folks think that the wilderness is a quiet place just because there aren't any folks around, but that ain't so. The woods have their own special sounds, and the lowlands speak different than the mountains, which agin are different from the river bottoms. It is when things get silent with no sound at all, that you sit up and notice, and try to get the hackles down off the back of your neck. Then, in the distance I heard a baying of dogs, and it sounded a little bit like Haskins' blue tick in the lead, but it was probably just my heebie-jeebies. Nevertheless, I was off and gone over the ridge, and down the mountainside, through the mists, and into the deep shadows of the valley. Once there I began to walk slowly, spending as much time stopping to listen as I did moving.

Along about grey light I came upon a lonely cabin on the steep hillside, sitting up on underpinnings with the back about two feet off the ground and the front about six feet off the ground. There didn't look to be any dogs about, so I crept in under the porch and started to scrabble back under the house when I barked my knees on some of the sharpest rocks I ever had the privilege to meet. Gritting my teeth, and trying to walk on all fours, I worked my way back, anxious about snakes, but tuckered out, cold, and needing to find a bed.

I sat there for a while, hunkered up and nursing my bleeding knees, then I guess I dozed off, because I woke to a yapping down in the ravine and found that the moon had gone down. Soon I could see a carbide lantern bobbing in the dim grey light just before dawn, as some coon hunter and his dogs came winding up the slope in my direction. I thought, "You idiot, don't you know better than to hunt for coons or possums up on the mountain? They're down in the bottom!" Then it occurred to me that they weren't hunting anymore, but coming home from a long night on the trail, and whoever it was lived here.

Suddenly the dogs were on me, moiling under the house, sniffing, growling, whining, and licking. I guess I smelled like them, because they never gave me away, but just settled down, tired and happy. One bitch lay close to me and took over licking my wounds. It sure was nice to meet someone that I didn't have to run from.

While I was getting acquainted with my bedfellows, a heavyset man with a beard thick and black as a bear came wheezing up to the front steps, heisted a gunny sack from over his shoulder and hung it on some old cotton scales hanging from a tree by the front steps. He took off his carbide lantern, set it on the porch still burning, plopped down on the bottom step, then reached behind him under the porch and fished out a jug. I studied his silhouette through the steps, wondering what I was going to do next.

He sat and tipped the jug for a while, and just when I thought he might doze off, he said, "You might ought to consider coming out, whoever you are. If I say 'Siccum,' them hounds are going to treat you like one of the coons I done brung home. Or I could just shine this here carbide under there and use my gun which I haven't unloaded. Or I could crawl under there and sit on you, which would be worse. What'll it be, stranger?"

I dickered with myself about trying to crawl out the back way, but figured a fellow that gabby with a person under the porch must sure be lonesome, so I said as I eased out, "It's just me, Lizzie Tackett, looking for a place to rest, so I can get away, come morning."

He creaked around, adjusted his center of gravity, looked me over by carbide lantern, and said, "I'll swan if it ain't a girl! I knowed the way them dogs wuz acting they had found an ally in their war agin poverty and pestilence—someone to steal a biscuit from, or someone to pull their ticks and mash 'em. Where you want to get away to ... or from, for that matter?"

I didn't get a chance to answer, because a woman in the house started in with a querulous diatribe, "Is that you, Billy Bean? Drunk and talking to yoreself agin? One of these nights I'm going to have to hunt you down in the woods, and find you've stumbled and fell on your own gun, and blown your foot off. I can hear the coons and possums now, laughing and slapping their tails against the ground, 'Look at Nimrod, the great hunter!' Quit talking to those mangy hounds of yourn, and come on in here and get in this bed."

I was just thinking how noisy it was getting out here in the woods, when from the bushes down the hill where the trail turned into the yard came a "Halloo!" It was a halloo from the stable of my nightmares—old Haskins hisself. He hollered, "Don't shoot, it's just a pilgrim, abroad in the dead of night, looking for his lost sheep." I reckon he spied me about then in the carbide glow and the passing of the night, for he added, "Aha, there you are, my beauty; I've found you, just like the pearl of great price!"

I might have been a pearl, but I didn't intend to be strung on his string, so I hissed them dogs on him with a low "Siccum," and out they boiled. Old Haskins didn't see which way they were coming from, so I reinforced my tentative plea with a positive, commanding, "*Siccum!*" They backed Haskins up against a tree, where he tried fending them off with his hat and whip.

Billy addressed the stranger and said, "Huh, you're the first shepherd I ever seen herding his sheep at night, and with a whip in his hand! Why didn't you corral 'em at sunset, so they'd be safe and you wouldn't have to be tromping around over the mountains in the dark?" With that my new friend Billy hied his hounds away, and waddled down to where Haskins was making his last stand, beating the air with one hand and trying to climb a cedar tree with the other. With a last nip the black-and-tans pulled back to flank Billy, and the bitch looked back over her shoulder at me to give me an encouraging look and wag. My kind of dog!

"Now is that any way to greet a Christian brother?" grumbled Haskins, while he felt of his britches to see how much the dogs had left him. "All I'm trying to do is find that there skinny-legged brat from Perry, plague take her! She done run off from her rightful appointed guardian! Stole a gunny sack of grub, too!"

I discovered this here rock in my hand, and having nothing better to do with it, I sailed it at that liar—hit him, too, and he went face down like wet overalls falling off a clothesline. Billy's jaw dropped, and he glanced around in my direction, then looked back at old Haskins laid out on the ground. He chuckled a little bit as he turned him over face up.

"Well, by gum, mister, you shore talked like a sorehead, but when you wake up you are going to be a bona-fidey sorehead; that is, if my night visitor didn't kill you." Turning to me he said, "Step over here so I can see what kinda wild cat I got—hiding under my porch, ordering my hounds around, and picking on my 'Christian brother.'"

I don't know what he saw in the gathering light besides a skinny, pig-tailed girl, tall for her age, with bloody knees and torn dress with graveyard dirt on it, wearing cast-off shoes from an older brother. I had my Ma's blue eyes and high cheekbones, and a perpetual tan from Indian forebears on both sides of my family. All he said was, "Humph! You look like a barked squirrel, but I ain't gonna pick you up and lose a finger for my pains!"

That's how I met "Uncle" Billy. And in the background, sorta in the balcony seat, that's how I met "Aunt" Maud. She had taken it all in from the window. She cackled, disappeared from the window, then appeared on the porch. She was in her gown, which must have taken three or four feed sacks to meet around her, and her hair hung in a frazzled brown braid down her back. She was big but she moved fast, and ushered me into the kitchen lickety split, saying, "Billy, get that carrion off the premises, and shut that stinky carbide lantern off while I fix this chile some breakfast."

CHAPTER THREE

L IVING WITH UNCLE BILLY AND AUNT MAUD WAS AN ANGEL'S WING FOR
me. Haskins never showed up around the place again for a long time,
though he did skulk around the Hollis store, which was west of us,
trying to dig up something on Uncle Billy. That didn't pan out too well
for him, according to Aunt Maud, so old Haskins dropped out of sight for
a while. Personally, if I had my druthers, I would rather keep a snake in
sight, than let it get lost in the grass.

Uncle Billy and Aunt Maud took and raised me like one of their own.
I guess they needed me the same as I needed them. Their grown son,
Woodrow by name, had left home, and was away in the Indian Territory,
looking for a place to take his bride-to-be, who lived over at Casa. They
were lonesome from his absence, and I guess that had a lot to do with why
they took such a shine to me. I had not got much personal attention from
my own pa and ma, what with all the other kids running around, and the
press of keeping food on the table and clothes on our backs. I missed all of
my family, but the memory of them gradually faded into a dull ache. Living
in the warm glow of Uncle Billy and Aunt Maud was like sunshine to me,
and I became a ray of sunshine to them. Most of the time.

One day while Uncle Billy was grinding his ax, he stopped, ran his hand through his beard, and said, "Waal, Lizzie, I've been in a deep brown study about you. I thought I would try to make a boy out of you, teach you how to hunt and fish, shoe the mule, and plant corn. Then I said to myself, 'What about teaching her to throw rocks, rassle, and chew?', and that brought me up short. I remembered that at our first meeting you introduced me to the niceties of rock throwing. I can't improve you none in that regard. As fer as rasslin' I can show you a couple of things to discourage anyone from getting too close to you. And chawing? I think we'll wait a while on that—you need to lose a tooth first, then mebbe you can aim like Aunt Maud. She's a real spitter, though she's for snuff, not chawing terbaccy. And I expect your own pa taught you how to ride, shoe, and plant. So that's out. I'll leave the fishing part to my Maudie, and maybe she'll teach you something you don't know about that sport. For my part that leaves coon and possum hunting, and the accouterments that go with it, like skinning and tanning the hides, cooking possum with sweet taters, and how to find your way home after a long night chasing all over creation. And there's a couple of other things that I do know— pitchin' worshers and huntin' crystal. You ever done either of them?"

Well, Pa and William used to pitch worshers every Sunday afternoon, but they said it was for the menfolks, so I spent my time playing dolls with Josie. Except that I did get the job of laying out the pitching holes, scraping the yard, and keeping the holes clean. It warn't like any of my other chores. Worshers didn't put anything on the table or on our backs either one. I will admit that scraping the yard did keep the ticks and chiggers from taking over the place, and it sure made it easier to clean up the chicken mess. But as far as knowing how to play, I allowed as I didn't have any firsthand knowledge.

As far as hunting crystal, I said that I didn't have any trouble finding them—they were the first things I had found when I crawled under the porch on that first night and cut up my knees. And I had seen them on every shelf down at the barn, as well as the specimens in every nook and cranny of the house. Crystals were pretty enough, though not too useful for chunking unless you had calluses all over your throwing hand. But for a grown man to spend his time scrounging around in the hills, picking up rocks? What use was that? I guess Uncle Billy read my thoughts, 'cause he said, "Now don't you sniff at me, you little runt. I'll have you know that there's plenty of fools in Hot Springs who pay good money for those crystals I take to them. In a couple of weeks, if you'll promise not to throw them at the squirrels, I'll take you on a crystal hunting trip, and if you can find me some smoky quartz, I'll take you to Hot Springs with me to deliver my next load.

"As far as worshers, let me explain that game to you. If you can chunk worshers as good as you chunk rocks, maybe you can learn the game. Git the hoe and let's clean off the yard."

After I scraped the yard, Uncle Billy drove a stob in the ground, paced off two paces, drove another stob, then paced off seven paces and two paces for two more stobs. I took his Pet Milk can and drilled out a can-deep hole at each stob, and smoothed out the lips. Then Uncle Billy laid out the side holes, saying, "These here holes are Yell County holes—over acrost the River they just have three holes at each end, all in a row. Here in Yell County we put four holes at each end." So saying he drove two more stobs a pace apart and halfway between the holes at each end. That made for a diamond of holes at each end. He reached in his bib and took out four worshers, the same kind that is used on wagon wheels, and small enough to drop into the mouth of a pint Mason jar. He handed me two. I didn't let on that I had laid out holes for my pa and William ever since I could remember. Uncle Billy was getting worked up, and obviously was enjoying himself.

"Now, Lizzie, watch me pitch these worshers. I want to slide them in one of those holes yonder. The nearest hole will count 'one.' Either one of the side holes will count 'two.' The back hole counts 'three.' Only holers will count, and if you put one in the same hole as me, they cancel each other out. Acrost the River they count a point for the one nearest the hole, but that's just because they can't hit the hole. That makes about as much sense as getting credit for every squirrel you almost kilt. Anyhow, in a game we pitch until somebody gets twenty-one points." Uncle Billy put both his worshers into the front hole, saying, "See! Now you try, but be sure you stay behind this back hole to pitch."

I hefted the first worsher, narrowed my eyes at the front hole where Uncle Billy's worshers had fallen, thought of that hole as a snake in the creek, and wound up to throw the worsher like a rock. Uncle Billy cried, "No! No! Not that way. Underhanded, you ninny. We're not trying to kill the hole, we're trying to lay the worsher in nice and easy."

I looked at him doubtfully. Then I tried a tentative sidearm wind-up like I used when I skipped "biscuits" with flat rocks on the creek. Seeing his frown, I decided to do it his way. They didn't go in, but they came close, one too soft and one too hard. Uncle Billy said, "I'm gonna leave it with you. You practice while I get the rest of the chores done down at the barn."

I got a can of worshers from the kitchen to go with the two I already had, and began practice in earnest. It was quite a distance from the pitching line behind one back hole to the other back hole, some eleven paces, but I got the hang of it pretty quick.

By and by I learned to put the worshers in whichever hole I wanted to, with hardly ever a miss. When I started "calling" my shots, Uncle Billy got so excited that he insisted that Aunt Maud come and watch, and would usually break out with, "Lookee at that country girl pitch!" Then he started working on my strategy, explaining that I must be careful about making a "two" or "three" when all I needed was a "one" to finish out my game. Then he taught me where and when to pitch a "dry" worsher so that I could block or frustrate my opponent. I could see that he was genuinely proud of me, and got almost as much fun out of me beating him, as he did in treeing a coon or possum.

CHAPTER FOUR

ELL, UNCLE BILLY MADE A WORSHER PITCHER OUT OF ME, BUT I STILL liked chunking rocks overhand. And when he took me crystal hunting, that's how I got hooked into becoming a rock hound. I still spend as much time looking at the ground as I do at the horizon, after all these years. It's had other benefits, too. I've never stepped on a snake yet.

One morning, just like he promised, we went crystal hunting. We took a nest of empty Tucker lard buckets filled with gunny sacking, a short-handled shovel, a rake with no handle, and a pry bar. Aunt Maud finished the load with a basket of the leftovers from last night's supper, and a quart jar of vinegar pie. I warn't ashamed of the food, far from it, but I hoped we wouldn't meet up with anyone. I could just see them looking at the collection of tools, and saying, "Uh huh! Sure you are!" when they heard what they were for, and what we were doing.

Meet up with anyone? I should worry! I don't think even the Indians ever went where we went—a place called Forked Mountain, out from Perry. To my mind, which I opened to Uncle Billy frequently, if digging was our game, then why not choose a spot where you didn't have to dig with one hand and hold onto a sapling with the other to keep from falling down the mountain? I guess he tired of my running commentary, because he told me to climb on up to the top and see if there were any outcroppings up there that had veins of quartz. I hied on up there, broke through the scrub of huckleberries hanging like a necklace around the mountain's crown, and found myself on a barren top, looking out on all the world.

Out of breath, I sat down on a boulder to admire the distant scenery, and daydreamed a little bit. But there's only so long you can sit on a rock in the sun without getting hot pricklies, so I began to look near at hand for a better seat. On the north side of my perch, the boulder had crumbled, leaving jagged protrusions. I bent down, picked up a fragment to look at, and as I did, it caught the light of the sun. I gasped, turned it in the sunlight again, agape with its beauty. Then I began scrabbling in the debris for more. If I remembered how Uncle Billy described the different kinds of quartz, then I was sitting on a treasure trove of smoky quartz, most of which was still anchored in the mountain. As I looked at the cleavage and cracks I saw that with some careful work, I could fill our gunny sacking and buckets in less time than it would take Uncle Billy to work up a good cud of tobacco. I started to let out a yell to Uncle Billy, but caught myself, and decided to pick up some of the best ones, which I wrapped in the gunny sacking and put in my bucket. Then I got an idea for some fun with Uncle Billy. I picked up a large piece of rotten shard, put it on top of my stash, and went back down to where Uncle Billy was digging, trying to keep my silly grin out of sight.

He warn't doing too good—I could tell from the activity on his face. But he had enough grace to ask me, "Waal, did you see anything up there? Or are you just wanting to go home?" I picked up the large shard, covered it in my fist, and then pulled a little crystal out of the sacking with my left hand. Kinda half-heartedly I said, "We might as well go home, there ain't nothing up there but these old dirty-looking rocks. See? Like this little one I brought you."

As he eyed it in surprise, I said, "Yeah, I found a big one the same color … not worth a hoot!" Then I let fly with my large shard, up, down and away.

Uncle Billy jumped, choked, swallowed his tobacco, and let go of the sapling he was holding to. He slipped and slid down the slope, coming to rest against a cedar snag. He finally choked out, "No! No! You ninny! Was that big one you just threw away a crystal? Lord-a-mercy! That was smoky quartz, you little fool!"

I set my bucket down where it wouldn't slide, and danced away out of his reach as he clambered back up to his former vantage point. When he had acquired equilibrium, he reached down to look in my bucket. When he looked in it, I thought he was going to fall again. I've never seen a grown man get so excited before about anything that warn't sinful. Then his face blackened again, "You threw away the biggest and best one? I can't believe it! I can't believe it!"

I said, "Come on, Uncle Billy, you didn't think I was that stupid, did you, acting like some fool boy? That was just a no-count rock I chunked. Come on up to the top—I'll show you something worth dancing about!"

We probably acted plumb looney up there on the mountaintop, cavorting around with each new acquisition, chortling and giggling. Then we sat down in the hot sun and ate every smidgen that Aunt Maud had fixed us. The joy of being the first gatherer of that nest of jewels had sort of mollified him, and he didn't upbraid me any for funning him. I did catch him looking at me sideways a couple of times, but when I would catch his eye, he would just look downwind and spit to keep from laughing.

On our many trips into the mountains, I learned from Uncle Billy how to patiently extract the crystals from the shard without knocking the points off. It was sorta like pulling a loose tooth. He could have been a dentist, and a painless one at that, as quick and as sure as he was with the crystals.

He taught me where to break a cluster off, and when to spread wider and get a larger mass out. I learned to poke around the exposed roots of trees hanging onto the side of mountain gullies, where crystals were often popped loose from the underlying rock. I learned to clamber down the ravines from an exposed quartz outcropping, looking for isolated crystals washed down by the rains. Sometimes we would take a hound with us, to sorta scout out those places that promised to be snaky. Mostly, though, we left them home with Aunt Maud, 'cause Uncle Billy didn't want them tearing up their feet digging in that sharp rocky ground. My feet got to be tougher than a hound's, and I didn't see the whites of my fingernails till I was nearly a grown-up woman.

We made several more trips to Forked Mountain, each time with too many buckets and too much sacking. It was hard to use discretion—our eyes and imagination were always larger than our ability, and we ended up gathering more crystals than we could carry. So we cached some of them in remembered spots on the way home.

Since I was spry and all, Uncle Billy sent me back by myself to get two buckets that we had cached. It was getting close to time for us to go to Hot Springs. Uncle Billy had other "business" to tend to, which is as good a way as any to describe his moonshining operation. He never did take me to see the still, and I never asked him any questions about it. Didn't need to, really—I had lain in the bushes across the ravine and watched too many times to have any questions. I could have run that still blindfolded.

I had left the mule at the store with Jim, Mister Cunningham's darky, and went on up the mountain alone. I remembered him from Ma's burying. He reminded me, "Miz Lizzie, yo' be careful, 'cause there lots of snakes out this time of the year." I already knew how snakes get aggravated at having to crawl all the way down the mountains to find water, and a sore-bellied snake is apt to strike without warning. Since the streams had just about dried up, I kept my eyes peeled.

I worked my way through the pines, then the scrub growth, before getting to the huckleberry patch. Aunt Maud had made me promise to take an extra bucket to tie around my waist so I could bring home some huckleberries. That I was willing to do, because huckleberry pie is the best pie in all the world. I know some folks think a berry is a berry— blackberry, dewberry, blueberry, or even possum grapes, muscadines, or whatever. I like them all, but no pie can hold a candle to huckleberry pie. Save your possum grapes for jelly; I'll give you a blue ribbon there.

It was hot and still, so I said to myself, "Get the misery out of the way early—get on up the hill and find those cached crystals, then to the patch to gather berries, then home in time, maybe, for Aunt Maud to make a pie before bedtime."

I found the crystals without any trouble, and turned back to the huckleberry patch. I try to pick the berries that hang underneath; they are sweeter and bigger. But picking them down low like that keeps you from seeing a bear in the patch with you, practically standing over you. I'm not sure who saw who first, but I do know which one of us screamed first. There was no way I could have got away from that bear if he wanted to follow me, but I guess a bear's brain cavity is larger than most folks think—it's not much of a choice between juicy huckleberries and a scrawny, screaming kid. Smart bear!

Out of range, I slowed down and shut off my screamer. Then I realized that I had not jettisoned either one of the crystal buckets, although the unlidded huckleberry bucket tied around my waist had lost about a fourth of its contents. That made me mad, but not mad enough to go back up the hill. I looked around and found some stragglers growing in a meadow, filled out my bucket and headed for the store. Jim gave me a lid to replace the one I had lost on the mountain, but didn't say anything about the two buckets that had lids, other than to opine that those other berry buckets "shore did look heavy" the way I was carrying them. I didn't say nothing, just sniffed. I didn't want Jim to think I was looney like Uncle Billy, the rockhound.

Next day (still full of huckleberry pie), Uncle Billy and me separated the crystals into various piles, according to color, point perfection, size, and clustering. I began to see how someone could get hooked on rock hunting. After wrapping the individual specimens in some black cloth that Aunt Maud had, we packed them into bundles for transporting. I was ready for Hot Springs, but we still had a week to go. My daily routine was to wash down the porch and sweep the chicken mess off, then sweep and scrape the front yard, and dress up the worsher holes. I asked Aunt Maud for extra chores to help fill the afternoons until we could leave for Hot Springs. Time was passing porely.

CHAPTER FIVE

INALLY, THE DAY CAME. WE SAID 'BYE TO AUNT MAUD AND WENT WEST through Hollis, then on down south, leaving Fourche Creek behind. We spent the first night at some campground that had a spring of water in the middle that smelled like rotten eggs. A lot of people were camped around it, but I didn't see anyone that looked like a crystal buyer—just a collection of large families, and none of them with a decent enough rock thrower in the bunch for me to challenge.

The next day we went on down the valley, and then around the bend we came upon this beautiful town, the biggest I had ever seen. Of course, it was the only one I had seen, other than Dardanelle and Atkins. Perry didn't count. I don't even grace it with the name of "town" now.

I had never seen so many stores and houses and stables and saloons all in one place, and I thought my eyes would fall right out of my face, the way a guinea pig's is supposed to if you pick him up by the tail. I had never seen such fine, dressed-up ladies and gentlemen, not even at Easter, and there warn't a church in sight. We stayed in the main part of town in a bathhouse called the Crystal Rose, and I thought Uncle Billy was addled to spend good money just for us to spend the night laying on our beds, listening to all of those strange sounds, and no breeze to blow through the room.

By the time the sun was up, Uncle Billy had given me instructions to make the beds, spread the black cloths on them, and set out all the specimens while he went downstairs for a spell. My stomach was growling, and I began to wish I were home, or at least loose so I could explore the town and maybe find something to eat. Looking out the window I saw this ditch running right down the middle of the street, with board bridges across it every so often. Then across the bridge right below I saw Uncle Billy coming. He had what I hoped was a sack of vittles, and was accompanied by a brace of men and a couple of women. They were dressed fancy, and seemed to be excited. I thought one of them would fall off the bridge, trying to get around the others and up alongside Uncle Billy, cupping his hand to hear what he was saying.

I heard them creaking up the stairs, and I had things ready when they came into the room. Their eyes went straight to the bed, but mine went straight to the sack in Uncle Billy's hand. I hung in the background eating these sweet biscuits shaped like fat worshers while Uncle Billy wheeled and dealed. It's nice to be where everyone is happy.

We finished about the same time. I wiped my mouth about the time Uncle Billy let them out the door. I was full once again, Uncle Billy was sitting on the bed, grinning big, counting the money. The visitors were gone, floating on a cloud, thinking they had taken the country yokels for a cleaning.

Uncle Billy said he was going to take a bath, and finally left me to do some exploring. I was a bit puzzled as to why a grown man would want to take a bath in the middle of the week, but I was too ready to see the town to bother with oddities like Uncle Billy and his bathing habits. I'd done had a bath the day before we left the cabin, and I had on a new blue cotton dress Aunt Maud had cut out of the not-so-worn parts of one of hers. I even had a little scrap of blue ribbon tied on the ends of my two pigtails, and I felt as fine as one of the crystal-buying ladies.

I lit off down Bathhouse Row, looking in all the windows at the Art Emporium, the Select Lady, and the Old World Art Gallery, and finally stopped in front of the Opera House. Not knowing what was in there, I waited my chance and snuck in. It was full of people, and was dark, except for the far end where the lights were shining on a full-fledged fight between a man with a whip standing over a woman kneeling on the floor with her arms upstretched, and half her clothes torn off. It was a good thing I didn't have a rock, or I would have taken care of him. Suddenly, some man came out of nowhere and grabbed the whip, knocked the bully down, and helped the woman to her feet. Then the darkness around me exploded with clapping and yells, and I realized that it must be make-believe. What a thing for grown-ups to be doing!

My head was still spinning as I broke for the street. I felt better in daylight where I could see behind me. Returning to the art gallery, I went in and headed for the corner of the room where there was a place to sit. I didn't know whether to focus on the pretty painted pictures hanging on the walls and sitting on easels, or on the people wandering through the displays. Luckily I chose the latter. They were having an auction, and I had to keep moving around to find a place where I could see. While I was listening to the auctioneer, I noticed this vaguely familiar headbone with big ears sitting on the second row, and thought, "Now who could that be? I don't know anybody in this town." I shrugged it off as probably one of the gents who had come to our room to buy crystals.

I turned my attention back to the auctioneer. He was holding up this powder horn which had a worn-out blackened thong on it, and a musket that looked like a first cousin to the powder horn. The auctioneer was saying, "Now, ladies and gentlemen, to close out today's auction, I have a most climactic treasure to show you. What I have before me, and feel unworthy to hold in my bare hands, are the weapons of one of the early pioneers in this country. I have it on good authority that they most probably belonged to Sam Houston. We do know that when he was passing through here on his way to Texas, that he was in the doldrums from losing his sweetheart back east, and got in a card game near here, and lost these to some cardsharp. This is a genuine piece of American history, and I am going to put these on the block and see who will open the bidding."

Something was bothering me about those relics. I moved up the side aisle to see better, and shore enough, they were what I thought they were. The powder horn had the initials "JNT" burned on its side, and the gun had a split cherry stock held together with some imbedded metal bars. It also had "JNT" burned into the stock. I suddenly knew why they looked so old—and so familiar. They had been through a fire…they were from my burned-down homeplace! They had been my Pa's!

I laughed out loud, and piped up, "Mister, you don't know what you're talking about. That there gun and powder horn belonged to my Pa, and to my Grandpap before him. American history, my foot!" I was almost up to the front by this time, and had half turned to face the audience. That's when I saw the front side of that headbone and ears—it was old Haskins! I'd never seen him without a hat on before.

He stood straight up, and with a face like thunder, pointed his finger at me and shouted, "Grab that kid! She's a runaway from her legal guardian, and has come to this city of sin, hiding from the law! Don't let her get away!"

Well, he called me a runaway, and that's what I done. It was too far to the front door, past all those staring people, so I dodged behind a potted plant, turned over a stack of painted canvases onto the floor, and fled for the rear of the establishment. One or two men joined Haskins and started after me, but they made the mistake of trying to plow through those canvases. I think I heard the first one rip, and then the agonized screams of the auctioneer, the owner and his helpers. I was looking for the rear door, but threw a backward glance to see one group trying to get after me and another group trying to protect their masterpieces from getting tromped on.

I finally shot out the rear door, which looked onto an alley that had a mountainside right up against it. I hesitated from running left or right, afraid I would get hemmed in. Instead, I climbed over some piles of trash, and started up the mountain, using my hands to grasp one sapling after another, like I done when I climbed up Forked Mountain with Uncle Billy. Sure enough, I heard men calling, "Block off the ends of the alley, she can't get away!" I found a rock under my knee, and having nothing better to do with it, I let it fly. It landed on the tin roof of a lean-to shed beside the Emporium. Someone sang out, "Hyar she is, over hyar in this shed. Come on, we've got her!" I sat and watched them "get me" for a minute, then crept on up the mountain. It leveled out onto another street, and I took off like a scalded fox in the direction of the hotel.

Uncle Billy was back from his bath, and was taking a nap when I burst into the room. "Uncle Billy, come on, we've got to get out of here!" I cried, panting. "Old Haskins is after me agin!" Uncle Billy didn't exactly sit up—it was more like he levitated out of that bed. He looked around wildly in the dim gaslight, then focused on me standing there big-eyed and scared. Then, as the words stopped rattling around the room, he sat back down, put his head in his hands and said, "Why don't you just go and scream at him? That'll stop him or anybody else from coming near you." With that he flopped back on the bed.

Well, I stood there with my back against the door staring at him for what seemed like a long time, thinking about the scene at the Opera House, and what Uncle Billy had just said; then my conniving mind got to working. I stayed in the room the rest of the day, working me out a little plan.

The next morning, while Uncle Billy paid up at the bathhouse, I stood in the lobby, thinking about how to locate old Haskins. For once I wanted to find him, instead of him finding me. When we stepped outside, Uncle Billy said he was going down to the livery stable and settle up. He gave me some money to pick up some of those sweet round biscuits called donuts at the restaurant. He told me to meet him at the upper end of Bath House Row, and we would start for Dripping Springs.

I didn't think I had enough time to find Haskins, much less do anything about him, but decided to give it a try. Knowing how tight-fisted he was, I skipped the deluxe places and walked along looking in the windows of the cheaper breakfast places. I don't mean I walked in front of a place and stood there like a picture for him or anybody else to see. I snuck up to the edge of the window and peeped in, slow-like.

I found him easy at the third eating place. He still had his big ears on, and was facing away from me. I checked around the corner of the building to see if it led to an alley, which it did, and then led back to the street. Good, I could outrun him, circle the building and not get boxed in. I checked on him again, and he was still working through a big pile of vittles, so I took my time, looking up and down the street for some likely witnesses. And there, just coming out of the hotel down the street, were two couples. The ladies had parasols and balloon skirts. The gentlemen had on fancy hats, and each one carried a swagger cane. When I felt that they were near enough, I stepped in front of the window and started a steady tapping on the glass, and waited until Haskins turned around. He had a napkin tucked under his chin, and was halfway to his mouth with a forkful of food. When he saw it was me, he sputtered, spit out his previous deposit, jumped up, upset the table, and the race was on.

I lit out down the side alley, slowed at the corner to make sure he was coming, circled around the back side of the building, and headed back toward the street again. There I turned on my screamer, and ripped at the neckhole of my blue dress, tearing loose the careful stitches Aunt Maud had made. Just as he was about to catch up to me, I jumped out in front of the two couples. The men stepped forward in defense of their charges with half-raised canes, but I dodged around them to take refuge among the balloon skirts, crying, "Don't let that nasty old man touch me again! Please! He kissed me and tried to tear my clothes off!"

Haskins plowed to a stop, but before he could throw out his "runaway orphan" speech again, those two ladies had joined in the screaming, and the two gentlemen were whaling him with their canes. They got him down on the ground, refusing to let him say anything, until up trotted a policeman. The last I saw from my vantage point behind the skirts of my protectors was the policeman hauling off a protesting and purple-faced Haskins in the other direction.

My protectors in skirts fussed over me and pinned my dress back in order, and my rescuers with canes took me in the restaurant and paid for the donuts I was after. Then I beat it for the livery stable, where I found

Uncle Billy impatient to be gone, holding the mule by the halter. I had such a sweet look on my face he scarcely noticed the rip in my dress. "By gum if I bring you agin, Lizzie, if you don't come when I holler for you. Where have you been, down at the Opera House teaching the ladies how to scream?"

CHAPTER SIX

OODROW CAME HOME EARLY ONE MORNING ABOUT A WEEK AFTER WE got back from Hot Springs. Aunt Maud had just put the cornbread in the woodstove. Uncle Billy was already down at the barn fooling around, and I was getting the tools ready to go out with Uncle Billy to hunt crystals. The hounds gave a preliminary barking, then broke into a delirious dance around this tall stranger coming up the path with a gunny sack over his shoulder. It had to be Woodrow. He was tall like Uncle Billy, but not as big across, and he had all his whiskers shaved off. He had Aunt Maud's light brown hair and greenish eyes. We sized each other up, not speaking, and then Aunt Maud swept into the yard and gathered Woodrow into her arms. I was a little embarrassed, so I went to draw a bucket of water.

Uncle Billy heard the commotion and came up to the house. He made proper introductions, and told the story about old Haskins getting thrown in jail in Hot Springs, and the time on Forked Mountain when I discovered the smoky quartz and fooled Uncle Billy. I felt like I was coming down with the ague. Woodrow sized me up again and said, "I think you'll do all right for a sister." Then me that can walk through the dark woods and dodge every hole or tripping root, had to go and trip over the front step in broad daylight trying to get the water bucket up to the porch. I fled for the rear of the house, mortified, trying to distance myself from the gentle laughter of Woodrow and Uncle Billy.

That week was a happy week, listening to Woodrow tell about the Indian lands west of us, talking about his girl Gracie and their upcoming marriage, about a life of freedom from the heavy sharecropping and toil that most folks knew in that part of Arkansas, about a freedom from clannishness and hatred. I automatically thought of Haskins, Cunningham and Robbins, wishing I could go too.

Woodrow left for Casa the next Sunday, taking the mule, and promising to come back by and let us see his intended before they got married and left for Hot Springs on their honeymoon. My brothers were scattered, and I hadn't seen them in over two years, so it was easy to look at Woodrow and feel like he was my brother, too. At times I even thought of him as something more than a brother. I talked to the dogs about that something fierce, saying that if that Gracie was no-count, I'd make it up to Woodrow, somehow. After all, I was going on ten, and big for my age. I could hunt and fish as good as any boy.

We thought Woodrow and Gracie would be back to the home place about Friday, but on Wednesday evening up came Woodrow on a lathered mule, pale and shaken. He slid off the mule, stumbled on the front steps, and fell into Aunt Maud's arms. Alarmed, Uncle Billy came running from the barn, and I hurried to get a dipper of water for Woodrow.

He told us he had got to Casa all right, and had a good visit with all of Gracie's kin. He said, "We was funning around, me and Gracie, down at the railroad trestle, and I says, 'Come on, Gracie, sing that favorite song of mine again. You know, the one about the Everlasting Arms. Watch your foot there, you'll trip and fall plumb into Fourche Creek, and then where would I be? Without a bride, that's where I'd be. Come on, I'll race you to the house.'"

Woodrow said that as they ran back to the house, Gracie got tangled up in her skirt and fell. He doubled back to help her, saying she would have to do better than that if she didn't want to get scalped out in the

Indian Territory, but when she didn't bridle at him, he sorta tapered off, thinking he had hurt her feelings. But her feelings weren't hurt, she said, she was just woozy. She went to bed early.

During the night, they called Woodrow in from the loft where he was sleeping with the boys, saying, "Gracie's sick, and she is calling for you."

Woodrow said he went into the bedroom to hear Gracie moaning and saying, "Mama, I can't breathe! I'm so hot … is this love? Will I really be married on Sunday? Mama, I'm scared. What if I really get sick? … Have Annie bring me a gourd of water, Mama, I'm so hot. I see arms, Mama, and there's Woodrow, sweet Woody … Woody, why do you look so mad? I haven't done anything, have I, Woody? Mama, where are you? Why have you all got a fire going in August? What is everyone looking at me for? You're as pale as a skinned catfish … Mama, I'm hot, so hot!"

My heart froze with Woodrow's next words: "Ma, she died, just like that! I've lost my bride. I've lost my Gracie!" He lapsed into a bitter keening and slumped down on the porch. One of the hounds put up a howl, and the others slunk under the cabin. Aunt Maud tried to fix something for Woodrow to eat; neither Uncle Billy nor I dared to say anything.

Woodrow was quiet a minute, but when he looked up he began to mutter under his breath, half singing, "What a fellowship, what a joy divine, leaning on the everlasting … banisters of Hell … moved to meet thee at thy coming … and they cry peace, and there is no peace … dust thou art and to the dust we return this body, Lord … safe and secure from all alarms, leaning on the everlasting banisters of Fourche …"

Aunt Maud broke in saying, "Woodrow, what ails you? Ain't it enough that Gracie's gone, and you set there muttering till the wick is burned out? Do you think Ole Man Trouble is new around here? Your Pa, he always said it comes in bunches, and it do, it do. Turn that wick down 'fore you go blind staring at it. It's plumb unnatural, son. Cry, if you want, but please don't set there staring at the flame with the dance of it in your eyes. Son, are you hearing me? You got yore old blue tick so upset, he's hackled up with sowbelly scraps goin' a-begging."

Woodrow got up and came on into the house, and never said another word. He left during the night, taking the mule. I warn't asleep, so I saw him go. Could I have stopped him? I don't know. What I do know is that I didn't try. Woodrow, we learned later, rode back to Gracie's folks, put the mule in the barn, and then disappeared.

Gracie's kid brother came a couple of days later to ask us to come. When we got there, some boys from across Fourche were there, babbling something about the crossing. Me and them lit out for the creek, with the others bringing up the rear. There was Woody—or what was left of him. He had met Engine Nine on the trestle during the night, and been knocked into Fourche. As the men pulled him out, I was sitting on the bank under a tree, out of sight, with my head between my knees, retching through my tears. I stayed there for a long time after the grownups had carried Woodrow up to the house. I watched a big old catfish circle around under the trestle, roil the water as he searched for his departed feast, then slowly swim away.

Well, after they buried Woodrow, Uncle Billy and Aunt Maud needed me more than ever, and I sure needed them. Aunt Maud would want me to stay at the house and help her with the hominy, or lard, or molasses, or with the canning, or the quilting. Uncle Billy would want me to bring his dinner to the field, sharpen his ax, go squirrel hunting with him, or ride the mule in. I was getting worn thin trying to be a comfort to both of them. In the evenings we would sit on the porch, them rocking, and me pulling ticks off the hounds, each of us with our private grief. One such evening Uncle Billy said, "Lizzie, why don't you and Aunt Maud go fishing tomorrow, mebbe catch us a good mess for supper?"

I perked up at that. Next morning after the chores I dug some worms down at the barn with the manure fork. They were just waiting for me, lying on top of the hardpan and underneath the manure. I filled a couple of Prince Albert cans, gathered up the fishing poles and some entrails, and Aunt Maud and I set off for Fourche. I hoped getting fish would be as easy as getting worms.

We found a nice shady spot near a deep hole that had a drift at one end, and a clump of willows in the shallows at the upstream end. After catching a mess of perch on my worms in the willows, we settled down in a likely spot near the log jam and tried to see into the depths of the pool behind it. We put some chicken entrails on our hooks and sat down to watch and wait. After a while Aunt Maud shifted her ponderous bulk to the other buttock, brushed the pine needles from her feed sack dress, and said, "Lizzie, watch now, that ole chicken gut is gonna get us supper yit."

My cork slowly sank an inch or two in the water, bobbed up vigorously, then sank decisively, moving laterally toward the flotsam just in front of the logjam.

"Easy, Lizzie, hush now…just a tad more…now, sock it home! Holy Moses! Don't break yore pole! He's done wrapped around a snag, plague take it!"

Not quite. It felt as big as a snag, but under the surface, some primeval brute—tough through many a spring rising, dimly puzzled by the tug of half-remembered battles with a decade of trot lines—chose to take my chicken entrail to the depths. My hook had struck home in his boot-tough mouth, and the war was on!

"Aunt Maud! Aunt Maud! Look! Help! I got one!"

Slipping and sliding, I hung onto the pole as the water turned to froth. Aunt Maud lumbered in my direction, saying, "Lord-a-mercy, Lizzie, we don't got us a supper…he's got us! Now when he surfaces and heads this way, run him around there into the shallows." Aunt Maud had sunk into the mud on the bank, and had to watch me haul in my prize by myself. I couldn't do much more than keep the fish from getting back to the deep water, so I waited until Aunt Maud had got her feet back under her, and together we hauled that leviathan to higher ground. There we found a sapling which I cut with my pocketknife, and strung that fish through the gills, so we could carry him between us.

As we labored up the slope, Aunt Maud said, "It ain't fittin', somehow. This belly-cat has torn the trot lines of every man in Yell County, and here we go toting him home. Look at us, did you ever see ary a sight?

You, skinny as a rail, and about as tough, but still a pigtailed brat. And me, who ought to be gracing my dogtrot in my rocking chair, or leastways, stirring the hominy pot. Here we are, waddling along in Fourche bottom with an overgrown catfish, looking like two spies from the Land of Canaan. Lordy, this 'un must weigh nigh ninety pounds. Now that's a bunch of grapes, eh, Lizzie?"

I was shifting the make-shift pole to the other shoulder, when I looked up the trail. We still had to get past the sumac clump, through the blackberry patch, over the rotten cottonwood carcass, then up the shaley path to the cabin … and there stood the shadow of an upright bear. Forever frozen in my mind, it was the bear of previous meeting at the huckleberry patch, Ole Ase of Forked Mountain, sniffing the air, and shaking his head as if to expel some wayward gnat in his nose. I dropped my end of the pole, screamed and headed for Aunt Maud's skirts.

I peeked around Aunt Maud's skirt and saw the bear lower down to all fours, and lumber off into the bushes. Then in the distance I heard Uncle Billy calling, "Halloo thar…Maud…you thar? …Maud? Tarnation, where is that fool woman? Hey, there's Lizzie sounding off agin … wonder what she's treed now? Iffen her ears wuz bigger, I'd make a coon dog out of her. Hie thar, Blue, whar you going? Come back hyar!"

Uncle Billy stumbled on down the path and came around the fallen cottonwood and there we were. He burst out again, "Lord-a-mercy, woman, what are you doing? Hush, Lizzie, you think I'm a bear or somethin'? Lizzie, I said 'Hush!' Woman, hesh her up, will you? Lord-a-mercy, what you got here?"

Uncle Billy slapped his knees with both hands and hollered, "Whooee! Look at this! It's Ole Hawg! I seen him in last spring's rising, that's him, couldn't be another like him from one end of Fourche to the other. Lost a line to him myself, I did. Ole Hawg, look who done caught you, a screaming kid and a fat woman, O how the mighty are fallen! Breathe, Ole Hawg, you'll last a bit yet. But come dark I know where you'll be— tumbling in the washpot! Tarnation, woman, how did you ketch him? Wish Woodrow was here now. 'Member how he haunted that creek year in and year out, fishing for Ole Hawg?"

Later that evening I came back into the kitchen after supper to clean up the dishes. Grease was congealed in the platter, and a pile of bones was all that was left of our feast. I went out on the porch to scatter the cornbread crumbs for the chickens, when I heard the unmistakable sound of retching, and then drifting around the shed I caught the acrid smell of vomit. It was mingled with the acrid rage of cursing. I ran into the yard, and there behind the shed was Uncle Billy lifting his ax for yet another stroke into the sticky, pallid head of Ole Hawg. With every descent of the ax was mingled the soul-lost refrain of "Woodrow, oh, Woodrow!"

I ran back to the house and told Aunt Maud what I had seen. "Why fer is Uncle Billy carryin' on like thet?" I asked in confusion.

She just shook her head and said, "Hush, chile. Some things you're better not knowing. Go to sleep now. You're all tuckered out."

CHAPTER SEVEN

THEN THE ANGEL FLEW AWAY. AUNT MAUD WAS TAKEN MY THIRD YEAR there, soon after we got back from Hot Springs on a crystal-selling jaunt. We had been hunting for a bee tree, and Uncle Billy found a black gum that looked promising. We gathered buckets, gloves, netting, some pine knots for smoking, and followed Uncle Billy to the tree. When it fell to Uncle Billy's ax, an outlying branch knocked Aunt Maud's bonnet off, along with her netting. That angry swarm of bees took in after her. She got stung pretty bad, and I guess it affected her heart. Anyways, her strength went and she sorta lost her vinegar.

I had often wondered, when she and Uncle Billy were spatting around, if they loved each other, but when she hit the ground fighting those bees I never wondered again. Uncle Billy dropped his ax, flew to where she was thrashing around on the ground, beat at those bees with his hat and bare hands, and covered her as best he could with his body. I grabbed a double handful of dust off the ground and ran over and threw it on them. After a couple of doses of dirt most of those bees flew off. Uncle Billy picked up Aunt Maud—no small chore—and carried her down to the creek. I fell in right behind them, swatting at a left-over bee now and then.

Uncle Billy was as tender as I've ever seen any woman with a child. He bathed Aunt Maud's face and put tobacco juice wherever he could. I could tell he was heartbroken and scared. The black-and-tans were whining and trying to get close so they could lick Aunt Maud.

Toward the shank of the evening, she rallied a bit and then began saying the same thing over and over: "Lawd, I thought I wuz tougher than thet!" Then she died, just like that.

Like most mountain folks, Uncle Billy and Aunt Maud were right private. Aunt Maud's funeral was private too, just Uncle Billy and me. Right after the funeral, held by Uncle Billy hisself, he went up the steps into the now-empty dogtrot, and I stood in the yard wondering what to do. It looked like, in his grief, he was turning away from everything. The jug sat under the step untouched. The black-and-tans were walking around like they had arthritis, plopping down to lay with their muzzles between their front paws, staring at the house. I started for the barn, thinking I would do the milking, when Uncle Billy came back out on the porch, and called me to help him get the mule saddled.

"I'm going into Hollis, and I'll be gone tonight," he said. "You stay here, sleep in the house, and stay on the place. Won't nobody sneak up on you with the black-and-tans here. I've done took that shotgun down from over the door so as you can reach it. Shorely if you're half as good with it as you are with a rock, you'll be all right."

Well, he was as true as his word. I thought he had gone into Hollis to find company to drink his sorrow away, or maybe to get Oren Blasingame to carve a tombstone. But there he was next day, on that mule—and riding double. Behind him was this yellow-haired gal that didn't look much older than Woodrow. You could have blown me over with a feather when he said, "Lizzie, this here is yore new Ma, and she's gonna be yore teacher, too!"

I sure wish he would've told me what he was doing ... I could've saved him a lot of grief, and me too. Her name was Hettie, and if I ever get me a pet wildcat, that's what I'm gonna name it. She was a school teacher from Hollis and she had citified airs. I don't have no use for airs.

It is hard to develop airs when all you know is hard work, ticks, chiggers, snakes, flood and drought, failed cotton crops, and fire-and-brimstone preaching. That's what most of us grew up with, and to meet someone with airs was a brown study.

But what really curdled my milk was she tried to teach them to me. If Uncle Billy hadn't been around, I would've been her full-time project. It was sort of a relief to see her working on him. Like when she decided Uncle Billy needed to quit chawing. She would worry-wart him from his morning chaw to his evening chores. He got so he would dig a hole with his boot heel before he spit, so when she brought his lunch down to the new ground where he was plowing, worrying out stumps, and burning brush, she wouldn't count the splatters. Then he got real subtle, and took to careful spitting, then putting a rock over it, but that ended after one of those rocks had a copperhead under it—it startled him so, he swallowed his quid.

He finally gave up chawing in exchange for her teaching me how to read and write. That is, except for his trips to Hot Springs to take another load of crystals. I would go with him just to get away from Hettie, and I swan if he didn't get a plug at every store, and hide them in the hay mow when he got home. One trip ended sorta like this:

"I suppose you bought you a plug, didn't you?"

"Well, yeah, I got one—it'll come in handy to put on wasp stings and sech." You never saw such an innocent face with such a black beard on it.

Uncle Billy could have disguised his tobacco in amongst several of his other aromas, but she wouldn't hear of it. Wouldn't let him in the house till he "bathed." She called it "bathing," but what she meant was "washing." She took it into her head that Uncle Billy ought to "bathe" every night before bed. Now asking a coon hunter to wash every night is ridiculous, summer or winter, rain or shine. Can you imagine tromping through the woods till past midnight, coming home to stumble around looking for the washtub in the dark, fill it with cold well water, lower yourself into it, then get out and have to look for a towel in the dark? Who would want to go coon hunting with that kind of reward? He finally wheedled Hettie into heating up a tub of water after supper, hoping it would still have some warmth by the time he got home. What that really meant was Hettie had me draw the water, heat it up and get it ready. Out of curiosity I checked the temperature on a couple of occasions to see how quick the water cooled. I might as well not have heated it.

Two incidents changed that routine. One crisp night I had just got solid asleep, when a roar broke out from the yard where the tub sat next to the washpot. Some snake had decided to swim around in that water while it was still warm, I reckon; anyways, he was laying there dreaming about summer and frogs when Uncle Billy lowered himself into the tub for his nightly ablution—the shortest ablution on record. I heard the water sloshing around, then Hettie threw up the window, and screamed, "What's the matter with you, William? Can't you take a bath without waking everybody within two miles?" Uncle Billy got ahold of that snake and in his panic flang it at the open window where Hettie was hollering. Unfortunately he missed it. The hounds had just got settled from their outing, but came out from under the house for a reprise. After milling around a bit, they found that stunned snake and made short work of him. They was about as noisy as Uncle Billy.

The other incident happened a short while later. It was a warm night for a change, and Uncle Billy lingered in the tub, experimenting to see if the jug alongside the tub had any effect on the water temperature. The moon had just broken over the ridge when he espied a polecat weaving around near the woodpile, cavorting with the cats on our place. I came wide awake to his loud whisper, "Get me my gun! There's a rabid polecat out here!" He was talking to Hettie, I guess, but that polecat thought he was talking to it. It turned its attention from the cats to Uncle Billy and wobbled over in that direction. I watched from my window as Uncle Billy contracted himself, legs (which normally hung outside the rim of the tub), arms and body into that tub, trying to get out of the reach of that rabid polecat. I could have rocked that polecat easy, but I didn't have no rock. The next thing I knew there was this ear-splitting racket as the gun went off—Hettie had decided to shoot from the window, rather than take the gun to Uncle Billy. Now when you don't know which way trouble is, you don't know which way to run. A gunshot in a mountain valley ricochets around, and its source is kinda hard to locate, especially when it is mixed with the reverberation of buckshot hitting a Number Two washtub full of water. Uncle Billy came out of that water like a duck off a winter pond, just in time to catch a well-directed spray from the startled polecat before it followed the cats into the brush. Those poor, overworked dogs wearily came out from under the house to take charge, some chasing off after that sweet trail through the woods, but a few stopped and cocked an ear and wrinkled a nose at Uncle Billy, who was giving an uncertain sound from his trumpet, notes those hounds had never heard before. I laid low and giggled myself to sleep.

Hettie made Uncle Billy's life miserable, but it was blissful compared to what she had in store for me. I thought I knew what hard work was, but I didn't until Hettie hove onto the scene. I sure found out. I also found out that I didn't have a servant heart, when she started treating me like one.

Hettie was a school teacher, and nothing else—she couldn't fish, cook, or wash. She couldn't make hominy, and she couldn't can. As far as I know, she couldn't quilt or sew. She couldn't even throw a rock. Well, you know where that got me—out on the delivering end of all those chores, which wouldn't have been unbearable, except that Hettie put on these airs about it being beneath her to do such menial work. That didn't leave me much choice; I would either have to give rein to my conniving mind, or else lay awake at night and fume.

It didn't take too much conniving. Hettie was mortal feared of any kind of crawling critter, and to bring up the subject was enough to give her the heebie-jeebies. So, one night at supper I asked Uncle Billy, "Uncle Billy, did you see that momma scorpion on the porch heading for the kitchen with about a dozen little babies strung out behind her?" I saw out of the corner of my eye that Hettie was listening with her fork halfway to her mouth, so I continued, "Uncle Billy, what's the furtherest you've ever seen a scorpion jump?" At that, Hettie's fork clattered to her plate, she jumped up, gathered her skirts, and beat a retreat to the bedroom across the dogtrot. Uncle Billy looked at me sorta calculating-like, but finally just grunted and gave his attention to finishing his cornbread and his fruit jar of sweet milk.

That is, he almost did. He slopped the last part, always the best part in my opinion, down his beard at the arrival of a blood-curdling scream from across the dogtrot. He jumped up, almost turning over the coal oil lamp, and roared, "What's wrong now?"

I jumped up too, trying to act surprised. "Was that Aunt Hettie, Uncle Billy?" 'Course I knew what had happened—I had done the washing earlier, and put the clean covers on their bed. A wail from the bedroom erased any doubt as to where Hettie was: "William, there's a scorpion in the bed! He just stung me on the foot!" While coming in from the clothesline with the bed covers, a corner of the sheet had drug through the grass burrs, and when I made up the bed, I found them. Throwing them away seemed such a waste. Hettie had found them when she slid down under the covers. While Uncle Billy stumbled to her rescue, I drank some more of my buttermilk, hoping it would eliminate my smile, if I was called to report.

Sure enough, Gabriel blew his horn: "Lizzie, come hyar!" I squared my shoulders, thinking that living in this house was good preparation for the Judgment Bar, and went across the dogtrot. "Lizzie, did you put some sand burrs or goatheads in the bed?"

Hettie interrupted Uncle Billy, wailing, "You know she did, there ain't any on your side of the bed. They're all on my side. She's just trying to pester me!"

I just looked at the ceiling, and didn't answer. Uncle Billy said, "Well, are you gonna answer me or not? Whut air you doing rollin' your eyes at the ceiling? You may have seen one of those angel paintings down at Hot Springs with all the cherubs staring up into the clouds, but it don't look quite the same on you." I let my eyes rove on across the ceiling until they rested on a spot just over Hettie. Then, just before I thought another outburst was coming, I pointed to the ceiling and said, "Lookee there, ain't that that momma scorpion?"

Hettie screamed and scooted over to the other side of the bed; Uncle Billy used his squirrel-hunting gaze and examined the ceiling. "I don't see nothing. It's too dark in here." I allowed as how I could have been mistaken, but I did see something move ... but it probably warn't nothing ... maybe. I volunteered to go get the lamp and help look for it, saying I sure didn't want them to wake up in the middle of the night with one of those scorpions dropping on them. I guess Uncle Billy was sleepy, because he said, "That's enough! Clean up the kitchen and bank the stove, I'm going to bed. Hesh up now, Hettie, I'm three times yore size, so if there are any scorpions around, three to one they will get me instead of you." I could see that warn't much of a comfort to Hettie, so I beat a retreat; kitchen chores sounded good.

I banged around in the kitchen, threw out the scraps to the hounds, turned the cat out, and went up to my loft. I lay there trying to smile myself to sleep, giggling a little bit as I thought of a scorpion jumping down on Hettie from the ceiling. At least, if I was a scorpion, that's where I would jump for a soft landing.

I reckon Uncle Billy warn't fully retired yet, because I felt the house shake a little bit, then heard a deep guttural "I got 'em!" It sounded like he fell down, then the house began to shake some more as Uncle Billy announced, "I still got 'im! Hit me, Hettie! Hurry!"

I said, "This I have got to see!" When I got down to their bedroom, there was Uncle Billy dancing around in his nightshirt with one arm clutching the back of it. He looked like he was trying to get a half nelson on hisself. His other arm was waving and directing Hettie. I got there just in time to see her obey her husband and swat him a goodly punch in the belly. "No! No! Not there, here! Here where I'm aholding it! Beat my hand—I've got him in my hand!" I stared open-mouthed as Hettie laid a rounder to Uncle Billy's back. It sounded like she broke one of his fingers, or maybe hers. At any rate he let go of his shirt and stuck his injured hand between his legs. Hettie moaned and rubbed her bruised hand. I watched a big centipede drop out of Uncle Billy's night shirt, hit the floor behind Uncle Billy and head for a crack in the fireplace. He must have been ten inches long, and he looked mad. Since my observations had already been rejected once, I didn't intend to make matters worse. Besides, they didn't see me, so I crept back to bed. That is, after I turned the covers back and looked carefully under the sheet and quilts.

Most of the centipedes around our place lived under the boards in the floor of the storm cellar, but apparently you never can tell where one will show up.

Next morning, we were finishing up breakfast, and I thought the temperature was kind of frosty, even though the oatmeal was steaming, so I tried to make conversation. "Well, did you all sleep good last night?"

Hettie fixed me with a suspicious stare, and Uncle Billy said, "Lizzie, when was the last time you was in the storm cellar?" I said, "Me? I hain't been down there since you sent me for those empty fruit jars. What ever did you do with them, by the way?" Uncle Billy sighed, looked over at Hettie, shook his head and mumbled something about being "enfiladed by the junior cavalry."

Hettie put me to work cleaning out the cellar later that day. But how do you clean a cellar that has a dirt floor with a couple of walk planks in it? I decided she hadn't ever been down there, so I gave some thought to praying for a fierce storm. There warn't many empty fruit jars left, and some of those had dirtdobber nests around the rims. While I was knocking those off and examining the black widow spiders that were entombed in the mud, I got the bright idea of looking under the floor boards. I was barefooted, as per usual, but that was no handicap—in fact, my feet were the toughest part of me. I figured if some crawlie were to come my way, I would rather feel it on my tough feet than to have it shinny up over shoes and socks to lay hold on some more tender part. That don't mean I was careless—far from it. I just didn't let things like that worry me since most of them weren't going to happen anyway.

The first board was sorta stuck in its own footprint, where it had been pressed down when the ground was wet. There were a few worms, not first-class ones like grows under the barn manure, but skinny, pale ones, plus one millipede and some clicker beetles. The next plank was warped a bit, so it was easy to get my fingers under the edge to lift it. I don't mean all the way under like a worm on a fishhook waiting for a nibble, but just at the edge ready to turn loose if discretion called. I lifted it and there lay a glorious pale yellow centipede, about nine inches long. He didn't move until I lost my hold on the plank while trying to hold it with one hand while I reached for a fruit jar with the other. Luckily, the centipede skittered across the dirt floor, and out of the way of the descending board. I chased it down with a stick and the open-mouthed fruit jar. In he went and I slapped a rusty lid on top while he furiously beat the sides of the jar. When he finished his dance, I screwed the lid a half turn, then looked around for another lid and punched a few air holes in it with a nail. After making a lid exchange, I stood there for a while admiring my new acquisition, and wondering how I could harness it to my conniving mind.

I had heard some discussion between Hettie and Uncle Billy about the centipede of the night before, so I knew I couldn't just right out fling it on the bedroom floor—that would be too suspicious, and besides, it would probably get away before Hettie saw it. Uncle Billy and the hounds were off in the woods somewheres, so I put my prize, along with some other empties, in an egg basket and took them around to the front porch. Hettie didn't come outside hardly any during this time of day, since she hated sun bonnets, and even more the idea of getting sun freckles. I duck-waddled around under the front steps, found Uncle Billy's jug, unstoppered it, and poured a swig into one of the empty fruit jars.

The Sunday before I had heard one of those visiting evangelists who travel through the mountains say that if a body would drink a little whiskey now and then he wouldn't have worms. I had given that some thought, but didn't think I had worms. Still, I wondered what would happen to a worm in whiskey, so I decided to pour a little in with my centipede and see what would happen—whether it would make him drunk, or change his color, or what. I guess I put in too much, or maybe it was the fumes. He woozied around like crazy, then keeled over and died ... I guess. I didn't get down close to see if he was really dead or just playing possum, and I didn't poke him with my finger. But he was mighty still.

Satisfied that he warn't going anywhere, I dumped him out on a cedar shake under the house, straightened him out to dry, then leaned back to study. It just didn't seem right to leave him down here by himself, so I took him around the house and put him in the kitchen on the woodpile for a spell. I heard Hettie go out on the dogtrot and get a gourd of water, then to the front porch and start rocking in Aunt Maud's hickory rocker. After she had set up a regular rhythm, I sneaked my trophy from the kitchen to the bedroom and deposited it under the edge of the bed next to the slop jar. I thought it best to let nature take its course from there on in.

Hettie was strictly a slop jar person. She dodged outdoor toilets like the poison. She also didn't like to get up at night in the dark, so invariably she had Uncle Billy get up to light the lamp at night when nature called. Not really a bad idea, with her fear of stepping on first one thing or another in the dark.

I excused myself early from the supper table, and as soon as I had the table chores done, I went to my loft. Across the way I could hear bed preparations being made. Uncle Billy had stepped out on the dogtrot to get his fresh air, then was the first one in bed. Hettie, as per usual, spent some minutes letting her hair down, brushing it out before the mirror. I could hear the scrape as she pulled the slop jar out from under the bed. She must have been on it several minutes, because silence reigned. Then the kingdom was overthrown, as Hettie focused on that odd shape just under the bed, about eighteen inches from her foot. She stood up, jumped back, and screamed all in one fluid motion.

Uncle Billy must have levitated, because I heard him crash back down on the bed, then sit upright, and thunder, "Lord-a-mercy! Woman, what is the matter with you?" I was peeking around the corner by this time, and Hettie was pointing with a trembling finger, which she used to punctuate her screams. Uncle Billy swung his feet out of bed and plunked one of them in the slop jar. He stood upright in shock, and beat a staccato on the floor with his new shoe, and with the last stomp he accidentally mashed the life out of that dead centipede. Hettie cried out, "O William, you darling! You rescued me just in time!"

Uncle Billy slowly extracted his foot out of its containment, surveyed the remains of the centipede, looked over at a couple of his curious hounds who had got up to see what had happened this time, and said, "Hettie, I think your idea about bathing before bedtime is not such a bad idea. I'll be back directly."

.

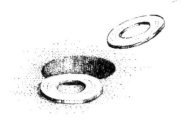

CHAPTER EIGHT

ETTIE WAS SUPPOSED TO BE MY TEACHER, BUT OREN BLASINGAME CAME up one Sunday afternoon, saying that they had a new teacher in Hollis, named Miss Blevins, and asked Uncle Billy if it warn't past time for me to be in real school. He also asked Uncle Billy if he "planned on being a bigamist, or could they count on keeping this teacher at the school."

So, at the tender age of ten, I started to school in Hollis. Most everybody else was from west and north of Hollis, so I didn't know anybody. But that didn't keep me from becoming acquainted with them. I was the oldest pupil in the first grade, and the other kids made sure I didn't forget it. The older kids taunted me with "Dummy" and "Injun", but I just sniffed and stuck my head in a book. Inwardly I boiled, and as I walked home I would give vent to my frustration by clipping off sunflower heads with a well-aimed volley of rocks.

I took two grades that first year, as did some others. Of course it warn't that we were so all-fired smart, but that we needed to get on through so we could do something useful, like pick cotton, can, or make hominy. Even so, Hettie made sure I never went to school unprepared, so Miss Blevins took a shine to me. She knew that the other kids were taunting me, and trying to make my life miserable. I told her not to worry about it, but I didn't tell her I was going to fix their wagon. Exactly where, when, or how I hadn't decided—but it was going to be done.

Spring rolled around and the marbles season passed, then the top season, and about the time the girls started playing jacks, it was time for baseball. I had watched out of the corner of my eye at all the boys' games, measuring and studying my tormentors. I was swinging "pepper and salt" for some of the smaller girls at recess one day, when a foul ball lofted over the screen and came arcing toward us. The boys hollered like they thought I was blind and couldn't see. I was swinging the rope with my right hand, and with the left I reached up and snagged the ball without losing rhythm. The catcher, Ted Gann, who was one of my tormentors, hollered, "Gimme the ball, Injun! And don't hit yourself in the back of the head trying to throw it." He came around the side of the screen smacking his fist in his mitt. I flipped the ball up in the air, shifted the rope from my right hand to the left, caught the ball in my right hand, and fired it straight at him. Hard. He warn't ready for it, and caught it right on the end of his thumb. Ted screamed, threw his mitt down, and stuck his hand between his legs in pain.

"What's the matter, Ted? Did I throw it too hard for you?"

Ted looked up through tears, saying, "I warn't ready! You tricked me."

I was heating up, so I fired back at him, "You couldn't catch it anyway, ready or not."

What followed was a volley of "Could too"s and "Could not"s. That escalated to a volley of "Dare you"s and "Double dare you"s. The bell interrupted whatever declension would have followed.

When I came out after school, ready to light out for home, they were waiting for me. Ted had his mitt, and the other boys were crowded around him, waiting to see what would happen. I walked by with my head high, and Ted said, "Hey, Injun, bet you can't beat me at 'hot potato.' "

I stopped and asked, "What's 'hot potato?' " As if I didn't know.

Ted said, "Here, you can use Chip's glove, and I'll use mine. Let's see who can throw the hardest."

"Well, what makes you think I'll take your word for it? Seems to me we will have to throw to the same person and ask him which one throws the hardest."

Ted answered, "No, you don't understand—we throw to each other, until one of us cries 'Uncle.' You afraid?"

"Nope, I'm not afraid. But how come you're going to use that thick mitt, and I will have this thin glove?"

"Aw, my mitt ain't thick, and besides, it's the only glove I've got. You can stick a hankie in your glove, if you want. Come on, I'll let you throw first."

I didn't intend to let him bruise my milking hand, so I decided to settle his goose early. I got out on the pitcher's mound, looked at the ball, giving it a few tentative pops in the glove, then said, "You gonna tell me when you're ready, or not? I ain't got all day, and I don't want to hear you saying 'I warn't ready' again."

Ted grinned, and spit, and said, "I'm ready. Pitch that ball in here, and if you can't throw it, roll it." I decided he was worth about three pitches, so I threw the first one as hard as I could, and it blazed into his glove with a loud pop. Ted jerked up, surprised and in pain.

I said, "Don't tell me you warn't ready. I'll throw it hard the next time so you won't have to stand around and wait for it." Ted looked worried, but he wound up and sent a hate ball my way. He was so mad he forgot where I was, I reckon, because the ball sailed far over my head and landed beyond the second base. I laughed, and said, "Hey, Ted, it ain't gonna do you any good trying to throw the ball away, 'cause I'm going after it. Jest a minute." I trotted back to the mound with the ball, held it up where Ted could see it, and let fire again. It warn't as hot as my first shot, but it didn't make any difference, because Ted was still stinging, and any kind of ball was going to make him hurt worse. I had thrown it straight at his belly button, so he couldn't catch it in the webbing, but had to take it in the pocket. I could see a sweat had broken out on Ted's face, and he looked pale. I said, "Are you going to throw it, or aren't you? Come on, time's a-wasting."

Ted's second throw was not as hard as the first since he was fighting to keep control. I caught it in the webbing of the shortstop's glove. I started to throw my third, then stopped and said, "Where do you want it? Hold your glove where you want it and don't move."

Ted said, "You're funning me." I replied, "No, I ain't! Put your mitt somewhere, anywhere, and hold it—I'm going to knock it out of your hand." It was pathetic watching Ted try one position, then another, anticipating how the ball would feel on his bruised hand in each position. He finally chose a stance that he thought favored his health, and waited. I burned the ball right into the pocket, without him moving a muscle. That is, until the pain hit him. He threw down the mitt, stuck his hand between his legs and whimpered like a beaten pup.

The onlookers had gotten deathly quiet. Finally, the pitcher, Dickie Fulmer, ventured, "Gollee! You sure do throw good. Why don't you play baseball with us ... Lizzie?" I looked at him, tossed him the glove, sniffed and said, "Why would *I* want to play a *boy's* game?"

I didn't have much trouble in school after that. Any kid that got picked on shined up to me and I became an adopted bodyguard. The girls didn't exactly fall over themselves being friendly, but I had put the boys in their place, so I was free from their snickering and gabbing. All the boys thought I was the Eighth Wonder of the World, according to a comment I heard Miss Blevins make about me to Oren Blasingame at the Pie Supper we had to raise money for a blackboard.

I didn't know what the first seven Wonders were, and I don't think any of us could imagine a blackboard as big as the teacher was talking about. Most of us used slates, but the teacher had heard about this big blackboard that would go at the head of the room, and be useful for teaching, so she had to have one. I think Oren wanted to talk about something else that night at the Pie Supper, especially since he bid and got Miss Blevins' pie, but all she wanted to talk about was this "educational tool."

One day about three weeks later a wagon drove up and stopped right in front of the schoolhouse door. We were all looking out the eyes in the back of our heads, trying to see who it was, and waiting for the teacher to lay into whoever it was for disturbing school. Miss Blevins marched to the door, which was open, gave a little scream and threw down her long ruler, and clattered down the steps. We bailed out and followed her. It was Oren, and he had something big wrapped in some quilts in the wagon bed. With Miss Blevins chattering away, and Oren giving directions to the rest of us, we all carted that blackboard up the steps and to the front of the school room. Oren spent the rest of the afternoon fastening that thing to the wall, and was still there making final adjustments when we left for home.

The next day we all filed into school on time, not a tardy one in the bunch. Miss Blevins was lit with an inner fire, which made me a little nervous. I admit that I didn't see the significance of that blackboard like she did, but even making allowances, I didn't see so much to get a-hissied over. After all, it warn't nothing new and earth-shattering like a new kind of foolproof animal trap, or self-stirring hominy pot, or even a worsher hole digger. It was just a big piece of slate.

Of course it warn't long before we discovered several things about that blackboard. It became our prime punishment. Whatever we did wrong, we had to write the correct answer a jillion times on the board. It took away our excuses that we didn't know what tomorrow's assignment was, because Miss Blevins always wrote our homework in the top corner of the board. If you were tardy, or talked in class, or broke the chalk, your name earned a special niche in the other corner of the board.

Having that "educational tool" warn't all bad though. It only took us one day to figure out that Miss Blevins couldn't watch us and write on the blackboard at the same time, so we learned to keep her peppered with questions about how to spell this or that, and how to do long division. During recess one day, when I had to stay in to write a zillion "I will not..."s, I was writing with a stub of chalk, which broke. When I scrubbed the stutter marks off with my hand, I discovered a delicious sound could be made if you held your fingernail just right. Tucking that away in my memory, I finished quick, so I'd have a little recess time before the bell rang.

But Miss Blevins called me back to the board saying, "Lizzie, this is for your own good, but I want you to look what you've done. The end of every sentence is drifting down on the right. Now erase those and try again, and keep your lines level." Since my memory warn't that deep, I didn't have to reach down very far to get hold of my new-found discovery. I erased the board vigorously, and at each down stroke I built in a trembling fingernail journey. I heard a scream, which startled me so much that I jerked all four fingernails across the board. I turned just as Miss Blevins screamed again, stamping her feet and covering her ears. I thought a scorpion must have stung her. It was amazing to see the fire in her eyes as she pointed a trembling finger at me, and shrieked, "Sit down! Get away from that board this instant! Oh! Oh!" I sat down.

Miss Blevins seemed to be getting more nervous every day. I wondered if it was caused by the blackboard incident, and started to talk to her at recess one day. I didn't get far. She shivered, moaned and sat down on the step, saying, "Don't! Don't. Please don't!" I went around the corner of the school house and cried, but I didn't ever bring the subject up again. I did talk to Oren about it, though. He said, "Lizzie, I know you didn't mean to, but some folks are just high-strung like that. They can't stand certain sounds. Even hounds can't stand a fiddle sound."

I was so ashamed that I couldn't look Miss Blevins in the eye after that. When she called on me to recite something I could make a tolerable job of it, although I usually looked at the floor, but when she called on me to solve something on the board I would mumble and beg off on some lame excuse or another. She probably knew what I was going through, but even the thought of talking to me about it would set her trembling. We were trapped, and didn't know how to break free. It was a miserable time, but God sent us a solution. No, I don't guess it was God, but anyhow, something happened to fix things right.

Ned Gorton was a little snot-nose who was always weaseling around to cause trouble between people. Miss Blevins had caught him at it on several occasions, and punished him every time. I reckon Ned went home and blabbed everything to his folks, because something sure lit a shuck under his Pap, Roscoe Gorton.

He came blazing into the schoolhouse one morning, stomping down the middle aisle, and stopping right in front of Miss Blevins. There were three of us still left standing at the blackboard in a spelling bee that morning, so I got a good view of Gorton. He had blood in his eye, and was brandishing a short whip. He thundered, "Did you whup my little Ned, or didn't you? If you did, I'm gonna give you a piece of my whip here. No hussy is gonna touch one of us Gorton men folks and get away with it."

Miss Blevins might have been highstrung, but she never flinched. She glared at him, and said, "Get out of my school house, and take your boy with you. He's already educated anyway. You've seen to that—he's just like you, more's the pity, and will never stand a chance to learn anything different."

I don't know whether Gorton understood that, or not, but he had come to thrash the teacher, I could see that. Before anyone could move, he reversed his grip on the whip, and cracked her over the head with the butt. Miss Blevins went down like a sack of meal. As Gorton drew the whip back to begin the whipping, I reached my hand behind me and scraped the board. The screech reverberated through the room, and Gorton stopped dead in his tracks. His jaw slackened, the whip clattered to the floor, and he looked with a pained expression in my direction. I gave the board another long and tremulous passage. Gorton groaned and ran for the door.

In a white heat I grabbed an ink well off the teacher's desk, and scooped up Dickie Fulmer's baseball off his desk and ran after Gorton. He had forgotten all about his boy, and had jumped in his wagon, trying to get distance between himself and that curdling sound from the schoolhouse. I took aim with the inkwell and let fly. It hit him in the back of the head, splattering what ink I hadn't got on me all over him. He turned around in fury, but seeing I had something else to throw, he bent over the horses and slapped the reins. I threw Dickie's ball with cold purpose. It caught Gorton behind the ear, and he fell out of the wagon, over the front wheel, and hit the ground, out cold.

One of the boys ran to the store to get Oren Blasingame. Dickie came out and retrieved his baseball, looked ruefully at the black ink stain on it, then at me. He shook his head in admiration, and turned to Gorton's unhearing form and said, "Strike Three, you're out!"

I ran back in and was holding Miss Blevins' head in my lap when she came to. She looked up at me with a dreamy far-away look, and asked, "What happened? Where is that horrid man?" I said, "I got rid of him, Ma'am. Don't you worry, he ain't gonna bother you no more."

Miss Blevins said, "But how? How did you get him to leave? He had a whip!"

I started to tell her, and caught myself. "Ma'am, it don't matter. He was just a little high-strung, that's all."

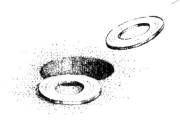

CHAPTER NINE

M Y NEXT YEAR OF SCHOOL, THE THIRD GRADE, STARTED WELL, BUT IT WAS doomed to be cut short.

Oren Blasingame closed the school. Or rather, he just shut down the school teaching. He and Miss Blevins were married before she even had time to get over the sore knot on her head. And we were without a school again. Not that it mattered—it was about time to break for crops, anyway. Which is why I was home that day in July, just before my twelfth birthday…the day that changed our lives for good.

I had finished scraping the yard, and had reamed out the worsher holes with an old Pet Milk can so me and Uncle Billy could have a good game or two. He had gone to "tend" to some things, which meant that he was at the still. I noticed that the locusts had wound down and either zoomed off somewhere else, or were looking up a new song in their songbook. It was unnaturally quiet, which, as I've said before, I don't like.

I heard a snick off to my right, down by the tree where the hounds had cornered old Haskins, and then on the other side, to my left, I caught a glint of reflected sunlight out of the corner of my eye. I decided it was time to gather up all the worshers I could, which I did, and said half out loud, "Whoeee! I'm shore thirsty," and moved toward the front porch.

"Stay right whar you are, kid!" said a rough voice. "There's three of us here, and we want yore Uncle Billy. Whar he be?"

I said, "Uncle Billy ain't my uncle. What do you want with him?"

The visitors had stepped out into view: one back behind me to the left under the bedroom window, the one doing the talking came out from behind a tree, and the third one, whose gun glint I had seen, came around the corner of the house by the kitchen. They were wearing black suits and dark hats. Now I don't like jaspers in suits. Especially when it warn't even close to Sunday. Suits is for city folks, undertakers, and preachers. I might make an exception for preachers. I remember Uncle Billy told me once about a banty rooster preacher who was holding a protracted meeting at the Hollis arbor, who strutted up to him in the yard before the services and said, "Brother Billy, I guess you think all preachers are jackasses, don't you?" Uncle Billy measured him, and said, "Naw, I wouldn't say that all preachers are jackasses ... just the ones I know." Well, that's how I felt about jaspers in suits. I jiggled the worsher in my throwing hand and considered.

The talking one said, "This must be the kid that Haskins told us about. Jed, you keep an eye on her, and I'll check the house. I 'spect he ain't here though, with the hounds gone, so he must be somewheres out there with them." He went up the steps to the dogtrot, stopped to spit a brown stream into my clean front yard, glared at me, then washed his mouth out with a gourd of water and spit it back into the bucket.

I thought, "When is that lazy Hettie going to wake up from her beauty nap?" The water polluter moved to the bedroom door, hammered on it with his gun butt, and stood back.

Hettie's whiny voice said, "Lizzie, is that you pestering me again? Why can't you let a body sleep? I'm going to thrash you as soon as I get dressed." I watched the man lean his gun against the wall, take off his hat, and announce with a silly grin, "That won't be necessary, Ma'am, you don't need to do neither one."

He reached for the door handle, and I pitched the worsher in my right hand at the "three" hole. It hit the ground and slid in just as pretty as you please. One of the men in the yard exclaimed, "Did you see that?" I sniffed a bit—after all, I warn't behind the line on that pitch.

"Hey, Jack, did you see what that kid did? That gives me an idea—what for is you the one on the porch, instead of me? Let's handle this in a sporting way. I'll wager this kid against yore pitching arm in a game of worshers. You win, and you can have the gal in bedroom; the kid wins and I get the gal in the bedroom. Elmo here can guard the door—he's not given to natural desires, so it'll be either me or you that gets the prize! How about it?"

All that palavering had finally brought Hettie to the window in her nightgown, where for a change, she had nothing to say; she just stood there white-faced, with her hand across her throat. Up to that time I thought I hated her, but a wave of sorrow swept over me as I saw her framed in the window. That picture has never left me.

Jack stared at Jed in annoyance, but grudgingly agreed, saying, "But we ain't scoring to twenty-one. These games are going to fifteen, and no more. I'm in a hurry for my prize!" Then he fixed Hettie with the hungry look of a bear espying a bee tree.

I knew that I couldn't afford to win, and I couldn't afford to lose. That meant that we had to come out dead even, and I didn't know whether I could do that. It depended on how good Jack was at worshers. My only hope, and Hettie's, was for Uncle Billy to come back. Sweat broke out under my arms, and my palms got sticky. The worshers felt slippery in my fingers.

If Jack made a hole, I had to match it. That I could usually do. But I warn't playing under ideal conditions. It gets touchy sliding past the two middle holes to hit the back hole, if that's what you were aiming for. It gets more complicated with an opponent's worsher laying on the ground just waiting for you to knock it in a hole for him. And then there's the arithmetic, keeping up with the score. I knew it would get touchy down toward the end, depending on who was pitching first. I had to work for a tie on either the first or second game, so I could control who won the last game. Winning I felt like I could do, and losing would be a snap—it was the tie game I had to sweat.

I didn't know where Jack was from, but he didn't seem surprised at my hole layout, so I guessed he must be from south of the Arkansas River. On the north side, at Atkins where I had gone once, they played by a different set of rules, sorta like horseshoes, and they only had two holes. That seemed like kid stuff to me. I liked Yell County rules better.

I found out early that Jack could pitch worshers, but I had him at a disadvantage—I was a kid, and a girl, and couldn't possibly be any good, plus he had on his suit. I lost that last advantage as we got well into our first game, when he stopped, bawled for a gourd of water, and took off his coat. I would have been glad to get him a drink, seeing as how he had spit in the bucket, but comforted myself with saying, "The heat gettin' to you, Mister?" He growled, threw the gourd onto the porch, and muttered something about a misbegotten squirt, which I took to be me.

We were at thirteen all, and he was throwing first. His worsher landed long enough but a half worsher wide of falling into the "two" hole. It was foolhardy, but I decided to see if I could clip his worsher into the hole, throw the game to him, then blow him away on the second game. In the heat of competition, I had forgot that I wanted to go for an early tie, so I let fly, and dang if I didn't clip his worsher right in the "two" hole and leave mine high and dry in front of the "three" hole. I stomped in fury, hung my head at Jed's lambasting, glanced up at Hettie still framed in the window, and looked sideways into the satisfied smugness of Jack's gloating sneer.

The second game was a breeze—I was mad. I threw five straight "threes" and won fifteen to nine. It was then that I remembered that the game was too short, and Uncle Billy just had to get here before the third game was over. Jed was gloating, and egging Jack, who was building up a thunderhead on his face. I figured I had better ease off or he would cancel the game, cook Jed's goose, and Hettie and I would be done for. It didn't take too much figuring to know that I warn't going to get out of this mess alive. If only that dang still weren't so far away!

Game Three. Since I had won the second game, I had to pitch first. I had to get in the second pitch position, so the arithmetic would be easier. I glanced at Hettie again, wondering if she was grateful that I had learned my ciphers, but she didn't have a ghost of an idea what I was doing. Oh well, not everyone can be skilled at conniving. Early in the game I began to play "hop-scotch" with Jack, letting him get ahead by a couple of points, then I would home in and push ahead of him by a couple of points.

After I tied him at nine all, we took a breather as Jack headed for the water bucket again. I dug him as he passed in front of me—"Gettin' kinda dry, Mister?"—which I shouldn't have done, any more than walking behind a mule in the barn, because he whammed me with a backhand across the mouth. I fell back against Jed, who was squatting on the ground in the shade. He shook me and pushed me back up, snarling, "Keep yore mouth shut, and get up there and win thet game!"

I wiped the blood off my mouth, cleared my head and went to the pitching line. Jack had just thrown a "lucky"—one of those rollers that roll and wobble around and fall in a hole. It had landed in the "two" hole. Jack was cackling, and slapping his leg. "Let's see you do that, you little brat!"

Well, I don't believe in luck; it's my thought that it only sets you up for a big disappointment, so I didn't let his lucky shot panic me none. It was still midafternoon, but it seemed like the temperature had dropped ten degrees. I looked at Jack, then Jed, and they were both sweating, so I knew that it was me that had gone cold, cold with fury.

I threw a "two" and tied him. Then Jack threw a "one." I threw a "one." He missed entirely. I smiled at him and laid my shot in the dirt. He threw another "one," and I matched it. Score was thirteen to thirteen. Jed interrupted the game at that point, saying, "Now wait a minute, what rules air you playing by? You're tied at thirteen. What if you go over the limit? Does that count, or are you busted?"

Jack looked with scorn at Jed, "We're playing Yell County rules—

fifteen wins this game, and nothing else!"

Well, naturally he threw short, way short. I laid my worsher right alongside his. He stretched, spit, and took careful aim. It fell dangerously close to the "three" hole. I laughed out loud, but away from his reach. "Getting jumpy, Mister?"

Jed was up now, cheering me on, "Come on kid, you can do it! Ram it down!" I laid my worsher right alongside Jack's, and Jed cried furiously, "You did that on purpose, you little bitch!"

Jack looked at me with slit eyes, weighing the possibilities. "Yeah, I believe you're right, Jed, she's trying to stall this game into a tie. Well, I'll just bury one and see if she can follow. All the pressure is on her."

He was right about that; he could relax and throw anything, and know I had to match it. He threw three more times, all misses ... I was getting hazy, but matching him on every throw. Then on his next throw he curled one into the "one" hole, and went to the shade of the porch, leaned against the rail, and said, "All right, my pretty, let's see if you can beat that. It won't matter, 'cause if you throw a "two" I'm going to break yore neck, and if you miss, Jed is gonna break yore neck. The rules just changed: This is yore last throw. How do you like them pickin's?"

I looked around at Hettie, who was crying, then at the house and the mountains, as if for the last time, then at Jack. "Well, Mister, you are the one that is going to have to break my neck, not Jed, 'cause there is no way you are going to beat me. I could've beaten you three straight, iffen I had wanted to. Which hole do you want me to put it in, the left or the right?" Not getting an answer, I said, "If it's all the same to you, I'll put it in the right hole. That's the one you haven't hit all afternoon." So saying, I buried it like it was my last worsher pitch in this life.

As it slid in, a shot rang out from the thicket, and Jack lurched back against the porch, bent over and grabbed his knee. Uncle Billy stepped into view with a leveled rifle, saying, "Waal, speaking of holes, thar's a hole in yore left knee ... would you like for Lizzie to put a worsher in that one too, Jack?"

Hettie screamed, I think. I fainted, I think. Anyways, I came to with a cold cloth on my forehead to see Uncle Billy and Aunt Hettie hovering over me. Looking through Uncle Billy's legs I could see the three suited jaspers tied to the cedar tree I always associated with Haskins. They had baling wire tied around their feet and wrists.

I looked at Jack with some malevolence as I stood up on wobbly legs, and said, "Air you ready for another game, Mister?" He cursed, but tapered off when Uncle Billy's rifle pulled up level with his smart mouth. Hettie took me in the house and tucked me into her bed. I could hear Uncle Billy talking in low tones outside, then he would get excited and talk louder, then explode with laughter as he recounted over and over how he had watched the entire game from the thicket. That made me mad, thinking of him in the thicket, and me and Hettie sweating for our lives.

I must of drifted off to sleep, because it was dark when I woke up. The lamp was lighted, and Hettie was sitting in a rocking chair beside the bed. She saw I was awake, and smiled. I asked, "Where is Uncle Billy, and those jaspers?" She shook her head and said, "Shush, don't worry about him, or them. He said he was taking them for a tour."

I decided I didn't want to ask any more questions about Jack, Jed, or that other jasper. I looked over at Hettie, who had this quirk at the corner of her mouth. She looked up at the ceiling and said, "Is that a scorpion I see up there?"

We both got taken with a case of the sillies, and from then on she was Aunt Hettie to me.

CHAPTER TEN

W E WERE LAZING AWAY MY BIRTHDAY AFTERNOON ON THE FRONT PORCH, listening to the locusts and hoping for a breeze, when the dogs perked their ears, sat up and then went down the front steps. They growled at first, then on signal from old Xerxes, our brindle, they commenced baying. Uncle Billy stood up, told Aunt Hettie and me to go in the house, while he found out who was coming to my birthday party. I could tell Aunt Hettie was nervous, and I had this sense of change coming, like a cloud on a sunny day, but knew there was no use fighting it. The clouds always pass. I was twelve years old today, so why shouldn't things be different?

Uncle Billy ordered the hounds in, and they retreated to flank the front steps, where they stood hackled and ready. Coming into view up the trail was a wad of men with hounds on leashes. I recognized two of them as Haskins and Cunningham, and the others I had seen around Perry, except for two strangers in suits. That didn't set well with me, so I crept out the back door and went behind the outhouse, or privy, as Aunt Hettie called it. I could see good there if I stuck my head around the corner, where I was screened by an althea bush. I could hear good from there, too.

The two strangers weren't very bright to my way of thinking, because they said right off the bat that they were working for the cause of sobriety and prohibition. Their eyes were kinda wild looking, and they were squinting like they would like to see around the corner. Moonshining warn't much talked about, but it was a part of life in our neck of the woods. For someone to barrel in and say they were going to sniff around other folks' business didn't seem too smart to me. They kept on talking and Uncle Billy let them ramble on. They bragged about how things was getting cleaned up in a lot of the States, and about how Carry Nation was coming to Arkansas to do some hatchet work on Demon Rum.

Then they allowed as how they were looking for three men they had hired to do some advance work, who, last tell they had, were headed up to see Uncle Billy. It had been a spell, and they hadn't reported in. Iffen Uncle Billy didn't mind, they would just take a look around and see what they could see. Uncle Billy said, "It's a free country, but who are those two jaspers there—what are they doing here?" He pointed at Haskins and Cunningham.

"Now, Billy, don't you go and get upsot with us," said Mister Cunningham. "We're just helping these here sober Christian gentlemen with their work."

Uncle Billy said, "Waal now, I'm sure we all appreciate your concern for crusading, but let me remind you that you're not welcome on this place, and that you will end up a lot happier if you will just skedaddle back to yore own business, before someone crusades into Cunningham's store, and finds a case of full fruit jars behind that stack of hemp rope in the feed room. You wouldn't want that to happen, now would you?" The two squint-eyed strangers in black swiveled their heads around to stare at Haskins and Cunningham.

Haskins fumed, "He's just trying to bamboozle us; ask him where that snot-nosed kid is, the one that rightly is my charge—I bet she knows something about those agents of yourn."

I somehow found a rock in my hand, but prudently decided to refrain from practice.

Haskins and Cunningham went into a conference, hesitated, then slowly turned back down the trail, muttering about the lack of Christian hospitality. Uncle Billy didn't even offer them a drink of water.

The agents and the others fanned out with their hounds and took off on several sorties, always turning back because of the steep, brushy mountain sides and stifling heat. There was any number of old trails crossing and crisscrossing all over the hills, but which one to take? I was fairly sure they couldn't find the still, but it worried me that they had hounds to track with, and Uncle Billy might have gotten careless.

I was trying to decide whether to creep back into the house when I heard voices—it was Haskins and Cunningham. They had left by the road, but apparently decided to circle back around the barn, and were creeping up to the outhouse. "We'll catch that kid or Billy's wife when they come out here, and we'll force the truth out of them, and get to the bottom of this mystery," said Cunningham. I held my breath while they slipped into the outhouse to hide. So far in my young life I had never been in an outhouse that smelled good, even one that had been abandoned for years, and this one got good use. It warn't but a one-holer, so it must have been crowded in there—and hot.

Like most outbuildings, ours had its own native occupants, among which were several fat yellowjacket nests. About this time of the year they are full, about to hatch out, and covered with protecting guardians, guns cocked and ready to fire. Unlike most people, we didn't knock ours loose, or singe them. There are worse things than yellowjackets, and they live in outhouses too—namely, spiders, and in particular, black widow spiders. They like toilets, particularly because they are real close to flies. They ain't many things that will hurry a body up like the thought, or even the reality, of a spider crawling on you where you can't see. That's why we left the yellowjackets to take care of the spiders. Since yellowjackets build their nests on the underneath sides of roofs, eaves, and such like, you can guess where their nests were. I found the stick that Uncle Billy kept behind the toilet to dislodge the nests on the ceiling of the outhouse (which were too close to his shaggy head for comfort), took a deep breath and held it, and bent down for a look-see. The rear of our toilet under the seat was wide open for ventilation, so I had a clear view. Carefully I poked a fat nest down, then quickly slipped around the corner and turned the wood latch, locking the door from outside.

What happened next was a delight. The avenging hosts swarmed up through the toilet hole to join battle with the two giants inside. I heard two erstwhile friends have a falling out, when failing at opening the door, they began to holler for help. Then I could hear each of them trying to push the other onto the seat as a plug. I beat it for the barn as Uncle Billy and several of the search party came running out to the outhouse. Uncle Billy is pretty quick with his wits; he probably recognized one or both of the voices within, so he called to the suited-up jaspers, "Boys, these may be your agents in here, you reckon? I ain't gonna open the door till you get here with reinforcements."

Uncle Billy turned the latch with a long stick, then hunkered down with the rest of the men as Haskins and Cunningham boiled out with a cloud behind them and made for the woods a safe distance away. I could see that the spectators were dying to slap their legs in glee, but restrained themselves so as not to attract attention to themselves.

All in all, it was a pretty good birthday party, though everybody felt like they had to be getting on home. The agents looked around one more time, saying "We'll be back." Uncle Billy turned to the swole-up Haskins and Cunningham, "And you, boys, will ye be coming back again soon?"

CHAPTER ELEVEN

E GOT SOME MORE VISITORS, BUT NOT TILL THAT FALL. IT WAS JUST after the leaves had fallen, leaving a beautiful carpet of color on the slopes. I was cavorting over the hills with the hounds, marveling at the undressed shape of the sensuous, rolling land. I had stopped to look down on our house far below, and saw that company had come . . . four suited-up jaspers. Aunt Hettie had gone to eastern Arkansas to visit her folks, but Uncle Billy was there. It didn't look like any of the Perry people had come this time, nor Haskins or Cunningham. I decided those two had finally decided to stay in Perry County where they belonged.

When I came up in the yard, they were all sitting there on the edge of the porch, and with their hats off. I could tell these were some kind of different breed. I sneaked around the side of the house and came onto the dogtrot from the rear. I gave them a careful look from behind, and saw that each had a bulge at his waistline, which hid their weapons, I supposed. One of them heard me, started, and turned around sideways so he could see what I was doing. "You must be Lizzie," he said. "Your Uncle Billy here has been telling us about you, but to tell the truth, I've already heard about you from a couple of your admirers over in Perry County. They don't have any proof, mind you, but they claim you have pet yellowjackets.

Is that true?"

Now that was a new twist! I moved onto the porch where I could look down and study him a bit before answering. I looked over at Uncle Billy to try and get some clue as to what was going on, but he sat still, not even rocking, looking out over the hills. "Tarnation!" I thought. "Does he expect me to handle this slick-tongued gent with the twinkle in his eye like I did the previous visitors? To say nothing of the three jaspers with him?"

I decided to play it straight, or at least as straight as a conniving mind can. "I don't know what you're talking about, but you must be referring to those jaspers who ruined all my late summer fish bait. You realize it's hard to come by worms this time of year, don't you? Anyway, they ain't no friends of mine, but it sounds just like them to try and pin their problems on me. Who are you, anyway?"

"My name is Kinsey, and I'm a federal investigator from Little Rock. These other gentlemen are from Hot Springs. We're here to investigate the disappearance of three men who work for a prohibition movement. They were last seen in Perry this summer, answering complaints about a whiskey still in these parts. I wouldn't say I have it on a good authority, though I thought so at the time, but we got a tip from some jaspers of local fame who go around crowding up people's outhouses."

He paused, looked at me narrowly, and then burst out, "I'll swan if I wouldn't have given a month's pay to have seen that!"

I looked at Uncle Billy again, and was shocked to see how old he looked. He felt me looking at him, turned and said, "Kinsey, I told you she don't know nothing about what happened to those agents, if that's what they were. Leave her alone. I'll go with you into Hot Springs. Just leave her alone."

One of the other jaspers said, "Shut up, old man, you've done all the talking you need do—save the rest of it for the judge."

Kinsey broke in, "That's enough, Hank. Just let me talk to this little lady a bit before we go. Lizzie, do you have any buttermilk in the kitchen? I'd be obliged to have a drink of buttermilk, I would. Let's go in the kitchen."

I said, "No sir, but there's some in the spring house. You can go down there with me and have some."

As soon as we got inside the spring house, I whirled and faced Kinsey. "What have you done to my Uncle Billy? Why are you taking him away? What has he done?"

Kinsey said, "Lizzie, sit down a minute and I'll tell you, but I have to ask you some questions. I want you to think before you answer; you be truthful with me and I'll be truthful with you. I'll even go first. You see, there were three bodies found a piece from here, buried in a shallow grave. Funny thing is they were all tied up with baling wire. That was a cruel way to die, for any man. Now I happen to have known all three of them, and they weren't worth much on my measuring stick, but they had a right to live—that is, unless there was a real good reason for them to die. Do you understand what I am saying so far?"

I sat down on the rim of the cool well where we kept the milk and looked at the ground, not answering.

"Now, what I want to know, Lizzie, is what reason could an old man like your Uncle Billy, who appears to be a gentleman, and loves you like his own daughter, have to do a thing like that? I have a warrant for his arrest on suspicion of murder, and unless you have something to say that we don't know, I imagine your Uncle Billy will be tried, and if found guilty, he will be hanged."

That story didn't really surprise me—I knew when Aunt Hettie said that Uncle Billy had taken them for a tour, that he had other plans. I had asked Uncle Billy once what happened to them, and his face gathered like a thundercloud, then faded into a look of the deepest grief I had ever seen. After that I never brought up the subject again. I would listen when he and Aunt Hettie talked of what was going on in the world—about the new "Rough Rider" President, or about our Arkansas Governor, but when prohibition came up, I always looked away and wouldn't meet his eye. He was carrying some deep secret grief, and I had had enough already.

I looked up at Kinsey, and said, "First off, tell me what all he has told you." When he was through I was appalled—apparently Uncle Billy had spilled my whole life out for these strangers to pick over, but hadn't said anything about the three men and their designs that day he shot Jack in the knee. I could feel tears coming, and suddenly I was bawling. Kinsey put his arms around me, saying, "Hush now, you're making it hard for all of us. Here, look me in the eye. There you go. Now let me ask you real slow, Lizzie, what was the real reason your Uncle Billy tied those men up?"

I told him the whole story, and he listened with a glistening eye, then a face of thunder, then he sank down dejected and sad. "You poor kid. I wish I thought I had half your grit and gumption. It's going to be hard, and it may not work, but I'm going to take you with me to see a judge in Hot Springs. He'll tell us whether there is a ghost of a chance of getting you on the witness stand. Your Uncle Billy is not going to go free, but if right is done, he is not going to hang. And you can be the one to save his life. How about it? Would you be willing to tell your story to the judge, and if he agrees, then tell a courtroom full of angry people, every one of which will remind you of your friends, Haskins and Cunningham? They'll try to get you flustered, accuse you of lying, say you're too young to be a witness, and that no one alive could do the things that you and Uncle Billy say you have done. What do you say, can you do it?"

I looked him in the eye, and said, "It ain't fair, but I can do it. Will Aunt Hettie have to go too?"

Kinsey said, "Hettie? That's Uncle Billy's wife, right? I should hope she will want to, but it's hard to judge what a woman will do when her husband is in jail or prison. She'll take care of you, won't she? Where is she, by the way?" I told him he could ask Uncle Billy, or he could wait at the train station in Hot Springs, because she was due in tomorrow afternoon.

We walked back to the house. I was wrung out like a dishrag, and I couldn't look Uncle Billy in the eye. Was it true that he had killed those three jaspers while they were tied up with baling wire? Somehow, that seemed to bother me more than him killing them in a fight. Then I thought of Aunt Hettie's face framed in the window, and realized that if push came to shove I would have no problem doing whatever it took to protect someone I loved. Carrying guilt for the rest of my life wouldn't be too high a price to pay for that kind of purchase. I just wished he had shot them in the front yard that day, and not later somewheres else.

Yet something still bothered me. I stopped at the front steps and looked at where Jack had stood on that day waiting for my last worsher pitch. I looked across the yard to the thicket where Uncle Billy had stood when he shot. And then it hit me. I guess it had been bothering me all along, but I couldn't put a finger on it: Uncle Billy could have nailed that jasper right through the heart or between the eyes if he had wanted to! A wave of relief flooded over me as I realized that he *didn't* want to, even with our lives in the balance. I looked up and met Uncle Billy's questioning look. "It's all right, Uncle Billy, I know you didn't kill them jaspers."

Kinsey was looking at me with a puzzled expression on his face, as if he intended to ask me how come I was sure about Uncle Billy's innocence, then thought better of it. He said, "Uncle Billy, do you have a neighbor who will take care of your hounds and stock while you're gone to Hot Springs, or more importantly, look in on your wife and this young lady, if you don't come back for a while?" It was the second time he had used the words "young lady," and they were both times about me. Nobody had ever called me a lady before.

Uncle Billy and I rode the mule, and Kinsey and his men collected their mounts from down the draw. We made it to Hollis in time for Uncle Billy to have a short conversation with Oren Blasingame about our stock and hounds, then pushed on towards Hot Springs. Dark caught us right outside of Dripping Springs, so we camped there.

Next morning Kinsey said that he and I were going to go right on into town and see the judge, and the others would take Uncle Billy to the jail. Things were happening so fast. I asked Kinsey if I could talk with Uncle Billy alone, and he said that it would be best, with a possible trial coming up, for him to hear what I said to Uncle Billy, and him to me.

"Uncle Billy, why don't you tell Kinsey here that you didn't shoot those three jaspers? Please!"

Uncle Billy looked at me with pain in his eyes, and said, "Lizzie, chile, it's over with and done. What those jaspers would have done to you and Hettie is deserving of death. Shooting is too good for such like. I guess that is what I intended to do with them all along when I led them away from the place ... I don't know. I had them all tied up with baling wire, and Jack weaseled out on his pledge. He didn't look like the Pussyfoot Johnson type to me, anyway. He begged for a drink of whiskey, so I decided to get them a jug from the still, and while I was gone maybe I could figure out what to do with them. When I got back they were gone. I thought about that a good bit, but couldn't figure out how they got that wire off so quick, and why the wire warn't somewhere on the ground, and where they were now. I sat down right there with my shotgun and finished the jug I had brought for them. No, I didn't shoot them, but I don't expect anyone to believe that. This here Kinsey says they were found in a grave on our place, and if they found them then I guess I can't deny it. If they are dead then I'm glad for yore sakes. You're safe from them, at least, though God knows there be plenty others in these hills just as evil. Whether I shot them or not, their blood is on my head.

"Come here and give yore ole Uncle Billy a hug before you leave. God gave me Maudie, and then Woodrow. I've lost them. Now he's given me the truest rock-throwing, worsher-pitching rockhound I've ever known, and she's a twelve-year-old filly. And now I'm losing you, too, but that figures—I've already had more than my share of grace. Let me give you this here smoky quartz I've carried in my pocket ever since the day you fooled me with it on Forked Mountain. Whenever I come to yore mind, Lizzie, pray for your Uncle Billy. Goodbye, Lizzie."

I still knew how to bawl, twelve or not, lady or not. I cried almost all the way from Dripping Springs to the Judge's house.

Just before we got there, Kinsey stopped, dismounted and lifted me down. "Lizzie, we're going to be at the Judge's house in just a little bit. I don't think it would be a good idea to see him with your face swole up. Wash up here at this stream and let's talk a bit before we go on."

After a long face-washing I got up and found Kinsey rubbing his chin, and absent-mindedly writing in the sand with a stick. "What do we need to talk about, Kinsey?"

"Lizzie, I was wondering. Do you remember telling Uncle Billy that you knew he didn't shoot those jaspers? I was watching him and he didn't bat an eye. Plus, I've been meaning to ask you, did you or Hettie hear any gunshots from up near the still? It's probably not far away, is it?"

I remembered that I was woozy and light-headed, but yes, it seems like I would have heard at least one of the shots. A shotgun makes a lot of noise. "What are you saying, Kinsey?"

"I'm saying that there weren't any shots to hear. Apparently neither you nor Uncle Billy know that those three agents weren't shot. Their throats were cut. Butchered like hogs, and still had the baling wire on their wrists and ankles. Now what does that tell you?"

My head was spinning. Not shot? Uncle Billy didn't know! Then he *didn't* do it! Then why wouldn't he say so? I guess Kinsey saw all those thoughts flashing across my face. He shook his head, saying, "I'm not to the bottom of this yet, Lizzie, but I'm with you. I don't think your Uncle Billy killed those agents. But he did tie them up, and left them there while he went for a jug. My thought is that someone came up about then, untied them and took them to that lonely hollow, where he tied them back up, and then knifed them. That 'someone' buried them in a grave shallow enough to surely be discovered. And that 'someone' also put a bug in Haskins' and Cunningham's ears to call the law and search Uncle Billy's place. Your Uncle Billy still feels responsible for their deaths, and in a way, he is. Come along now, I think it's time we lay all of this before the Judge."

I tagged along behind him, but all I could think of was that somewhere there was a "someone" with a bloody knife, and he was loose.

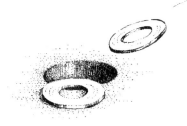

CHAPTER TWELVE

JUDGE BOUDREAU LIVED IN A TALL HOUSE ON THE NORTH END OF Bathhouse Row, with flowers cascading over the wall at the front gate. I remembered seeing the house on my first trip to Hot Springs with Uncle Billy, and thought then that the turret tower on the front with the stained glass windows must house the richest man in town. We climbed about a dozen steps to the front porch, and Kinsey rang a little bell hanging beside the door. Soon a huge black woman opened the door and looked us over. "'Morning, Miz Sammy," said Kinsey, like he'd been there before. "Mister Kinsey and Miss Tackett to see the Judge, if he's available."

She went off somewhere to tell the Judge he had visitors, while we sat in a side room that Kinsey said was called a parlor. It sure didn't look like any parlor I'd ever seen. I almost forgot what we were there for, as I feasted my eyes on what looked like a whole wagonload of furnishings in that one room. I had seen into Mister Cunningham's house from the outside, but this was far and away above that, plus I was actually inside, sitting on a horsehair sofa, looking at a massive square piano across the room, and running my feet over a real carpet on the floor.

Miz Sammy, who had let us in the front door, came back and ushered us down the hall to a dark room lined with books. When my eyes adjusted to the light, I could see an old man behind the desk. He had muttonchop whiskers, and had a pipe going, behind which I could see steely eyes measuring us.

He took the pipe out of his mouth and said, "Well, are you folks looking for a marriage license? If so, I might as well tell you now, I git to kiss the bride."

I was stunned. Was he joking? Since Kinsey looked stunned too, I figured somebody had to say something, so I did. "If that's so, I jest changed my mind about getting married, Judge."

The Judge busted out laughing, then Kinsey joined in, a little uncertainly. I sniffed and stared straight at the Judge. He took off his glasses and said, "I've already heard about you, young lady, if you're who I think you are. Didn't I see you staring at my house from the street a while back? And warn't that about the time I had to deal with a certain gentleman who was arrested for molesting a child in broad daylight down by the cafe? Your name would likely be Lizzie, wouldn't it? Your admirer, who said his name was Haskins, I believe, had quite a few things to say about you. I have even given some thought to coming up Hollis way to see if any of them were true. He didn't exactly compliment you, you understand, but I learned a long time ago to read between the lines. Have a seat, and tell me what can I do for you on this fine morning."

Kinsey laid out the story as he knew it from Uncle Billy, slightly embellished, but not much. The Judge stopped him several times to ask me a question, then would clear his throat, go to the window and stand with his back to us for a while. I thought he was thinking, but then I saw his reflection in the mirror, and it looked like he was about to bust out laughing again. When Kinsey got to the part about the baling wire, from then on the Judge got real attentive and serious. As I listened to Kinsey my heart sank. Who would believe a cock-and-bull story like that?

Judge Boudreau turned to me and said, "Lizzie, if this thing lands in my courtroom, as I see it, you are going to be asked some questions that may embarrass some folks. Decide right now to tell the truth. I'm talking not just about murder, and those dead jaspers, but other things too, like 'How many fruit jar customers did Uncle Billy have?' and 'Are any of them in the courtroom?' You may think you stirred up some yellowjackets up there in the hills, but answer those questions right, and you will see bees in every bonnet of this fair city! Not just the saloon folks, but the church folks too, and maybe even some of their preachers."

I said, "Judge, I'm just a country girl. I don't care what anyone here thinks about what I say. I just want to know where that jasper is who framed my Uncle Billy."

Judge Boudreau recommended a place down the street where Aunt Hettie and I could stay, up over a cafe. When Aunt Hettie got off the train in Hot Springs later that day, she was expecting to see me and Uncle Billy waiting there for her, but she was mighty surprised to see me standing there with a tall, clean-shaven stranger in a go-to-meetin' suit. We had to tell the story all over again, and by the time it was over, me and Aunt Hettie were both bawling. But when she was through bawling, she set her jaw and said, "Lizzie, we're going to get through this, somehow."

It plumb surprised me when Aunt Hettie took a job waiting tables at the cafe to pay for our lodging—the very same Hettie who'd never turned a hand at anything but school teaching. I cleaned rooms at a hotel owned by the same man who ran the cafe. I would sit close to Aunt Hettie after the days were done, trying to keep my thoughts off of someone with a knife, out there in the dark. Kinsey gave her a derringer, and told her to carry it with her at all times, even at night. Remembering her marksmanship with the polecat, I didn't get too much comfort out of her having a gun. I could've slept a lot better if Kinsey had given it to me.

The day of the trial came, and sure enough, it was just like Kinsey had said. Everybody jumped on me like chickens on the last junebug of summer.

A gaggle of women from a local church missionary society stormed into the courtroom the first day, refused to sit down, and stood before the Judge with parasols and Bibles in hand, haranguing the judge about the propriety of a "child" being subjected to such indecency. The Judge did a pretty good job with them, Kinsey told me. The Judge said, "Ladies, we are honored by your presence. But let me remind you, it is no more indecent for a child to venture into the citadel of law and justice, carrying nothing but truth, than it is for Carrie Nation to venture into a spittoon-festooned saloon full of rowdies with a masculine hatchet! She may do as much here for justice as your society has done for prohibition!" I got the idea that if he was an elected official, then he had just lost the next election.

It didn't end there. Some pear-shaped lawyer asked for the permission of the court to say a few words. The Judge said, "By all means, Mr. Bradford, sir. It will be the first time that this Court has ever heard you speak a *few* words."

Mr. Bradford harrumphed, and said, "As a friend of the court, Judge, I want to protest the appearance of this juvenile in court. Everyone knows that a young mind is highly impressionable, and this unlettered country girl is not going to be a reliable witness to the facts of the case. I sympathize with the disruption in her young life, but it will be a travesty of the first magnitude for the lives of solid citizens to be threatened by some wild story from an imaginative, over-heated brain. Moreover, the dignity of this Court should not be subject to a sideshow of these proportions. It's akin to ... to calling a Negro as a witness, or even a foreigner."

It was then that I realized the wisdom of Kinsey in giving the derringer to Aunt Hettie, instead of me. But if I just had a rock, or even one of those brass knobs off the railing in front of the jury box ... I looked over at Kinsey, and he sensed my mood, turning and whispering, "See, I told you."

Another lawyer, who was sitting by my old friend Haskins—I could tell he was a lawyer because I couldn't understand him—spoke, saying that he had heard of the so-called "worsher game," and that it would not be allowable in testimony, because all the adverse witnesses were dead. Judge Boudreau hammered with his gavel, saying, "That's enough! We'll have no reference to the facts which might bear on this case in this Court before it has seated a jury. Let me remind you whose court this is. Court is now called to session. Will the clerk please call prospective jurors into the Court."

The lawyer that Kinsey had persuaded to take Uncle Billy's case didn't want to talk to me. I heard him say to Kinsey that I was a liability, but I didn't know what that word meant. However, I did know what the lawyer meant. I kept my eyes on him pretty close from then on, and sure enough, during one of the recesses, I saw him jawing and laughing with the prosecuting attorney out in the hall. That didn't make me feel too good.

Like I said, I didn't understand what the lawyers were doing, except eating up time, but after a full two days of haggling, arguing and challenging one another they agreed upon a jury. Some of them didn't look too much different from regular folks, but they seemed to have put on special faces for the occasion. They were all men, white, employed, eager to be a part of justice. When they looked at Uncle Billy their eyes seemed to be cold; when they looked at Aunt Hettie, they looked too long to suit me; and when one or another looked at me, the corner of their mouth curled.

The prosecuting attorney made a lot, or tried to, of the fact that Uncle Billy had married so soon after his first wife's death. And that he had married a woman so much younger than he was. When Haskins got his turn on the witness stand, he made Uncle Billy the picture of a gun-happy moonshiner, uncivil to his neighbors and strangers, a holder of runaway children, non-churchgoing, and anti-Mason. Then along came Cunningham to back him up, adding that Uncle Billy had me in virtual slavery, without a chance to get any kind of learning. The prosecutor then produced some rusty baling wire, which he said had blood stains on it, and offered it in evidence. Some deputies were put on the stand to tell about their gruesome find in a shallow grave on Uncle Billy's place.

Then a retired clergyman was called, who said that he was a proponent of decency, law and order, and the "harbinger of a blessed day a-coming when Demon Rum would be dead." He was getting a little too thick, and the prosecuting attorney cut him off short. He didn't want the preacher stealing his thunder. After dismissing that witness, he "stripped the bag," saying that one of the great evils of the day was the production and sale of noxious alcoholic drink, and that its curtailment was a must to save the world from ruin. He was opining that it was that very Demon that had done the dastardly deed of murder through the lustful hand of a greedy and covetous hillbilly—Uncle Billy. Someone at the back of the courtroom gave a hearty "Amen!" Everyone turned to see who it was, and he stood to his feet, a burly man with a fanatic's gleam in his eyes.

The prosecuting attorney then called his next witness, and it was the "Amen" stranger. He said his name was William Eugene Johnson of Omaha, Nebraska. When asked his business, he said, "I'm on the trail of every bootlegger in this land, until liquor is stamped out! I have just come from the Indian Territory, and have had no small part in shutting down saloons and joints all the way from Kansas into those heathen Indian Lands and to the borders of this fair state. My enemies call me 'Pussyfoot' Johnson, and they are afraid of me—I use their lying, scheming, devilish tactics agin them, tricking and trapping them wherever I find them, in lodges, churches, homes, saloons, and restaurants." Even the prosecuting attorney looked at him a little askance after that outburst. "And do you have anything to say that bears on this case, Mr. 'Pussyfoot'?"

A song started floating through the window from out on the lawn, and people stopped momentarily to listen:

> *O Mister Johnson, turn me loose,*
> *Don't put me in that calaboose!*
> *O Mister Johnson, turn me loose,*
> *Let me have my Kickapoo juice!*
> *O Mister Johnson, what's the use*
> *Of pouring out all that joyful juice?*

Pussyfoot turned beet red, gripped the arms of the witness chair, then bolted upright, "Judge, and members of the Court, please excuse me, I've got some business to attend to." With that, the stalwart warrior rushed from the scene. Whether he caught his hecklers or not, we never heard.

Judge Boudreau kept waiting for Uncle Billy's attorney to make his move. Kinsey was looking increasingly frustrated. Aunt Hettie leaned over to me and whispered, "He's been bought!" It sure looked like it, or else he was the dumbest lawyer around. He monkeyed around with some papers on his table, and then tried some cross examination, mainly aimed at the retired minister, trying to work up some sympathy among the ones on the jury who just might not be teetotalers. I could see the Judge looking at Kinsey and me, wondering why I warn't called to the stand.

Instead, Uncle Billy's attorney called Aunt Hettie to the stand, not out of any strategy, but just so he and the jury could see her better. It worked out pretty good though, because she told the whole story of the worsher-pitching contest, culminating in Jack's getting shot in the knee. There was some tittering from those who thought it was just a made-up story, which I guess gave the prosecuting attorney an idea. Thinking that he could trip me up and make Uncle Billy's case look foolish, he called for a meeting at the bar, and whispered that he would like to call me as a witness, whether I was young or not. Uncle Billy's attorney protested, weakly, but at some unheard comment by the Judge, he relented.

Kinsey had a suppressed smile on his face as I edged by him on the way to the witness chair, and Hettie squeezed my arm as I passed her. After I was sworn in, the prosecuting attorney lit in. I had already measured him, so he didn't bother me none. He asked me to tell my side of the story, looking for a loophole that he could pounce on, I guess.

When I finished, he swallowed a smile, and said, "Now Lizzie, you don't expect me to believe that, do you?" I said I didn't expect much of anything out of him, and someone in the jury laughed out loud. That flustered him, and he said, "Nobody likes a smart-aleck kid, Lizzie." I guess that sounded good to him, because he followed up that comment by smacking the rail between us and thundering, "I've been watching you sniff your nose every time a lawyer speaks, or is mentioned. I suppose sitting up here in the witness chair like the high and mighty, and doing everything short of thumbing your nose at us, you probably think all lawyers are jackasses, don't you?"

I glanced over at Uncle Billy for permission, and said, "No sir. Just the ones in this room." The Judge coughed and spent some time hammering with his gavel, and when quiet was restored, someone else in the jury cackled, and the Judge had to do some more hammering. The prosecuting attorney said, "Judge, I demand that that last comment be stricken from the record."

Judge Boudreau answered, "Do you want it stricken because it's not true? If so, I guess your contention is that even the lawyers *outside* this room are jackasses. Clerk, strike the witness's comment. Is that all, Counselor?"

The prosecuting attorney reminded me of an old dog we used to have that wouldn't quit, even with hedgehog needles sticking out his nose—he just had to keep on trying one more time. He lined in on me again. "You young whippersnapper, this claim of your worsher-pitching ability is hogwash! Why, you couldn't hit a spittoon with your head stuck in it!"

Well, I was getting tired of being belittled and was wishing I had a rock, when I noticed that the brass knob on the rail beside my chair had come unscrewed and had somehow found its way into my fist. I stood up and yelled at him, "Mister, you see that spittoon back by the door?" Everyone turned to see what I was pointing at, when I let fly. That brass knob sailed through the startled crowd, and splashed into the spittoon with a majestic *kerplunk,* cascading tobacco juice on the bailiff standing by the door, and half a dozen spectators who were unlucky enough to not get a better seat.

People, including the prosecutor and the Judge, were stunned. The first to move was the bailiff, who started down the aisle toward me with juice running off his chin. Again, someone on the jury cackled. Judge Boudreau held up his hand, "That will be enough. Bailiff, you are temporarily excused. Counselor, do you have any more questions for the witness? If not, let me propose that we adjourn for lunch and reconvene on the front lawn croquet court. I, for one, am interested in seeing if this young lady can do what she and Missus Bean have described to us today. If so, then I rule that her testimony be entered as solemn truth."

Kinsey told me later that the Judge was completely out of order, and knew it, and all the attorneys there knew it, but no one questioned his pronouncement. Kinsey hugged me as I came down from the witness stand. I looked over at Uncle Billy, whose eyes were smiling even if his mouth warn't, and I could see him mouth the word, "Conniver!"

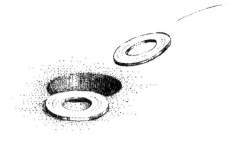

CHAPTER THIRTEEN

THEY REMOVED ALL THE CROQUET WICKETS AND DUG WORSHER HOLES AT one end, supervised by some old worsher experts in the town. The court was roped off, with chairs for the jury just inside the rope on one side, and the Judge and all the lawyers on the other side. I examined the holes critically, hefted the worshers, rejecting a couple in favor of some old ones worn smooth from handling. The Judge forbade anyone from standing at the end just behind the holes—I guess because he was nervous. Possibly he didn't believe the whole story either.

Judge Boudreau called the court back into session, reminding the witnesses that they were still under oath, then turned to me. "Lizzie, are you ready?"

I said, "No, sir, I can't do it." A murmur ran through the crowd, and Kinsey and Aunt Hettie turned as white as a new slop jar.

In consternation the Judge said, "Can't? What do you mean, 'Can't'?"

I looked him in the eye and said, "I need someone to pitch agin."

The Judge's shoulders sagged, and I heard him say under his breath, "You rapscallion!" Then he called for a volunteer from the crowd to pitch against me. Several boys stepped forward, but I said, "You ain't good enough," and they stepped red-faced back into the crowd.

"I'll play her," said a man back in the crowd, and he came forward to where I was. I looked him over, and decided by his chiseled cheekbones and tan skin color like mine that he was at least part Indian, which meant that he probably knew how to play. He said in a low voice to me, "You need someone to push you, don't you? You'll get no mercy from me, young lady, because I'm the best there is out in the Indian Territory where I come from. Let's warm up."

Actually, no worsher game was going to top the one I had with Jack, with so much riding on the outcome, but this one to prove that me and Aunt Hettie weren't liars had a different kind of pressure. I was still simmering from the hard time the prosecutor had given me, and was determined to show them all that a country girl could do as much as anyone else. The pressure was, as Kinsey told me during lunch, to make the jury realize that everything we had said was true so that they would be lenient with Uncle Billy. He didn't say it because he thought it would make me nervous; I knew he also meant it would give him more time to find out who butchered those three men and framed Uncle Billy. That man with the knife, whoever he was, had never left my thoughts, and I looked for him in every crowd without knowing what he would look like.

The fellow from the Indian Territory said his name was Keithley, and after our game he was going back home for a land rush that was getting ready to happen. He said the government was giving away some more Indian land that didn't belong to them, and he might as well have some of it, seeing he was half Indian hisself. I looked at him sharply, saw he had a humorous glint in his eye, and said, "Mister, I hope you git what you want, except for today."

He had about the smoothest, most nonchalant swing I ever saw, and he was good. I halfway suspected that he was better than I was, and would push me to the wire. We, like all good worsher players, shut the crowd out of our minds—it was just me and him. I threw first and decided to rack a "one-two-three" to see if he would follow, or try to get ahead. My "one" went in without a problem. I chose the right-hand hole

94

for my "two." Most people think you should aim for the "three" hole, since it counts the most. But the danger is that you really need to slide into the hole, and there isn't much sliding room behind the "one" hole to make a "three." Of course, you can live dangerously, and try to slide between the "one" hole and a "two," but most people, if they do that, choose either the left or right side and use that approach all the time. Then the day comes when you need to make a "three" to win the game, and sitting square in your favorite lane is your opponent's worsher, forcing you to try for the other side, or else hit the "three" on the fly. Because of that, I had learned to shoot from either side. I made the "two," and let Keithley have his turn. He followed my lead, and holed the "one," then holed the left-hand "two." I tucked that knowledge away, guessing that he liked to pitch around his opponent. It was my turn again. I slid a "three" in, again using the right-hand side, then laid my other worsher in the left lane to test him. Sure enough, he tried the right-hand lane twice, missing both times. I thought I had found at least one of his weaknesses. Now the game could get interesting as we tried to cat-and-mouse each other, but I didn't try forcing him to the right side any more. The spectators were choosing up sides, and I saw little side bets taking place. They began to cheer when a good throw was made. I had been used to boys jeering me all the time when I was in school, so noise didn't bother me. Keithley was having a time deciding how good a player I was, and whether I knew how to sucker an opponent. That is where I learned to be conniving, or as Uncle Billy says, I was a born conniver, and worshers just happened to come along.

We had agreed that there would only be one game, not the best two out of three, for the sake of the Court's time, and that we would play to fifteen instead of twenty-one. We were at six to three, my favor, so I decided to make my move. I laid a "three" in, using the right-hand lane, then plopped my second shot in the left hand lane. I thought I saw a look of irritation on Keithley's face. He tried for the "three" first, using the open right lane. He hung one over the "one" hole, then on his second throw he nicked it into the hole and left his second worsher stranded. I threw a "two," then slid a softie into the front of the "three" hole, about an inch away from dropping. Keithley studied that for a while, looked at me in suspicion, decided to play it safe and threw a "two" and a "one," which left him four points behind. I threw a "three," which put me at fourteen, so I ditched my second worsher, and watched to see what Keithley would do. He had no choice. He tried the left lane with both shots, making one "three." That put me ahead fourteen to ten. He could win with a "two" and a "three" if I missed both of my shots, or made something other than a "one."

It was time for the test. He was expecting me to sink a "one" and ditch my second. Instead, I laid both my worshers side by side in the left hand lane. Keithley said something in some Indian language, and clinked his worshers together. That was the first time he had done that, so I knew he was nervous. He was definitely a left lane player. He could have tried for the "two" hole both times, but even if he made them, he would still be at fourteen. He decided to go for the win. Staying away from the right hand lane he lofted his worsher for a "two" shot. It hit crazy, wobbled around and finally dropped in the "two" hole. I tugged at my pigtail as he got ready for his last shot. Part of the crowd was cheering him on; the rest were silent. Blocked out by my two worshers in the left lane, and afraid to try the right lane, he tried a "fly"—and it missed badly. It actually rolled through where the double wicket used to be. We looked at each other, then I stepped up and laid my worsher in the "one" hole, easy as you please.

The crowd whooped and hollered. Keithley and I walked over under the tree to get a dipper of water, waiting while everyone else hurried back to the courtroom for a good seat. Keithley took his worshers, and while I watched him over my gourd of water, he slid both his worshers into the "three" hole from where we stood, which was ten feet farther back than the pitch line, and he used the *right hand lane*. "That's for the spittoon, Lizzie." I saw the brown splatters on his britches leg from where he'd been standing too close to where the brass knob landed. I stared at him, and he winked at me.

"Come on out to the Indian Territory, Lizzie!" he said. "We'll play some doubles and make us a killing."

To which I replied, "Reckon I could, Keithley. After all, I'm part Indian, too!"

Keithley said, "It figures." He smiled and raised his hat to me and mingled back into the crowd. I lost sight of him, and hurried back into the courtroom.

As I slid into my seat Kinsey whispered into my ear, "Got you a new boyfriend, Lizzie?" I sniffed at him and stared at the empty witness chair. We all stood when the Judge came back in.

Uncle Billy's attorney, a little confused, called for Kinsey to take the stand. After being sworn in, and going through his relation to the case, he related his story about Uncle Billy and me both thinking that the three dead men had met their end by shooting. Because of that he knew that somewhere, maybe even in this courtroom, there was a murderer who had set up Uncle Billy to be the fall guy.

Uncle Billy's attorney did a sensible thing—he rested his case. The Judge said some things to the jury about 'a reasonable doubt,' and they retired to do whatever juries do when they are by themselves.

We were hopeful that someone on the jury would be persuasive for our side. When they came back in the late afternoon, it didn't look good. Everybody looked as mad as a wet hen. When the foreman stood and said, "Your Honor, we cannot reach a decision," it was the Judge's turn to look as mad as a wet hen. He pointed his gavel at them and said, "Get back in that jury room, and come out here with a decision!"

Well, they finally did. Bitter and sweet it was: ten years. But Uncle Billy was not going to hang. Kinsey would have time to ferret out the missing man with the knife.

Then the Judge called me up to the bench and said, "Lizzie, I've got some bad news for you. I don't like it, but I can't do anything about it— you have to be remanded to the custody of Haskins, who applied for your guardianship. The only sunlight in this sorry mess is that Haskins isn't married, and I have made him agree to let you be bound over to

Cunningham, who is. I wish you could stay with Hettie, but it's not possible."

I was stunned. I looked for Kinsey, but he was talking to Uncle Billy. Aunt Hettie had her head in her hands, weeping. Willing to run off to the Indian Territory, I looked for Keithley, but he had left before the court reconvened in the courthouse. I looked over at Haskins and Cunningham, who were staring at me with malevolent gleams. Uncle Billy saw my face, and tugged at Kinsey's sleeve, pointing at me. Kinsey came over and I stood there like a wooden Indian, telling him of my new destiny. His face darkened, and he hurried over to the Judge. After a hushed but heated exchange Kinsey returned to Uncle Billy with the news.

Uncle Billy hollered, "Haskins, you there, and Cunningham, you listen to me. I've never killed anyone and you know it. But if you so much as whup Lizzie, I'll come after ye, you hear? I may be old and gray when I get out, but I'll come after ye!" Then Uncle Billy broke down and they led him away.

CHAPTER FOURTEEN

ISTER CUNNINGHAM LIVED IN PERRY WITH HIS INVALID WIFE, POLLY, and her sister Sally. He ran his store about a block away to the west with the help of Miz Sally. I found out right away why he was so anxious to take me off of Haskins' hands. Mister Cunningham was tired of taking care of a whining and ungrateful wife, and wanted to get about his business of making as much money as he could, running the cotton gin and keeping the sharecroppers busy on his bottom land. My sister Josie had lived with them for awhile, but she disappeared one night, and rumor had it that she had eloped, and I sure didn't blame her.

All I had to do, he said, was take care of Miz Polly, which I found out included fanning, killing flies, emptying the slop jar, cooking and cleaning, taking care of the yard and garden, and washing the daily-fouled bed sheets. All Miz Polly had to do was think up some new chore for me to do. I would look up from my work in the back yard or garden, and see her laying in her single bed in the back corner bedroom, which had big windows looking out on the yard, clothesline, and garden. I could tell she was just working up the venom to scold me if I stood up to straighten my aching back.

If I did something too slow, or too fast, and was within her reach, she would swat me with her fly swatter. If I was outside, and the windows were closed, she would bang on the window pane with that fly swatter until she got my attention, and if the windows were open she would screech at me.

That was the negative side, but the positive side was that I had my own room, could eat all I wanted in the kitchen, and occasionally I was to get an allowance. At least that's what they told me. The first allowance came after my first month there, and was a nickel. I really didn't care about seeing Mister Cunningham or Miz Sally either one, so I stopped at the other store in town down by the railroad tracks and bought some gewgaw or other with that first earned nickel. That earned me an acquaintance with Mister Cunningham's razor strop. He said not to *ever* spend *his* money at that other store. I seemed to have forgotten that it was his money, even though he gave it to me. So I decided to save my next allowance, which was another mistake. When time rolled around the next month for another nickel, Mister Cunningham called me in to the dining room where they were eating supper, and said, "What did you do with the nickel I gave you last month?" I said, "I'm saving my money, Mister Cunningham." He thundered, "Saving it! If you've got so much money that you have to go and save it, and not spend it at my store, then I guess you have got too much money." That was the end of my allowance.

I also got to work at the store, sweeping and emptying out the spittoons and mousetraps each day. While I was finishing up one morning Miz Sally said, "Here, come here and hold this spool for me." She stripped off about a fourth of it onto an empty spool she had, snapped the thread and tucked it into the slot on the edge of the spool, slipped the paper wrapper back over the thread, and said, "There, that should be enough thread for any sharecropper to make it through the winter. Any more would be a waste."

I asked her, "Miz Sally, how much do you knock off the price when you do that?"

If I had been a plum when I asked that question, I would be a prune now. She said, "Gimme that spool! You better get on back to the house before Mister Cunningham catches you here. Don't you know that Miz Polly can't be left alone?"

Luckily, I warn't altogether alone in my indenture at the Cunningham place. Jim lived in the shed out back behind the house. I had known him nigh all my life, long before the day he helped dig Ma's grave. He was such a kind and hard-working fella, sometimes I didn't even notice he was a Negro. He did the hard and heavy work that I couldn't do, and also handled the sacks of feed at the store, and during cotton-picking time he had to clean the lint at the cotton gin. It fell to him to help me each time Miz Polly fouled her bed. He would throw this robe over her and pick her up like a baby, and I would jerk the sheets off and put on fresh ones. I made a terrible mistake about the fourth time we did that.

I was out in the garden that day just before noon, picking tomato worms and throwing them into the red ant bed, and Jim was down at the barn, giving the buggy another coat of paint. I heard Miz Polly turn on her fly swatter. I hollered at Jim to come help me, and said, "Coming, Ma'am."

Jim picked up Miz Polly, but I got in his way trying to get the sheets off. Miz Polly's gown slipped off her legs, and Jim tried to cover her up while holding her. She slipped, but Jim caught her just as Mister Cunningham came in for his lunch, and just as Miz Polly screamed, "He touched me! He touched me! That nigger touched me!"

Mister Cunningham whammed Jim alongside the head with his riding crop, and Jim staggered, but didn't fall, holding on to Miz Polly until I finished getting the sheets on. Miz Polly screamed again, "He's still touching me! That nigger is still touching me!"

Mister Cunningham hollered, "I'll teach you to lay a hand on my wife! Get out there in the back yard, nigger! I'll larn you!"

When it was over and done, I saw that I still had the soiled sheets in my arms. Mister Cunningham had ripped Jim's shirt off, tied his hands to the cross bar of the clothesline pole, and wore himself out whipping Jim with his buggy whip. There was blood on the grass, and red speckles on the windows to Miz Polly's bedroom. Mister Cunningham was plumb out of breath as he growled, "Next time, nigger, I guess you'll make sure that there is clothing between a white woman and your hands!" I looked through the doorway, and Miz Polly was up on one elbow, looking through the windows, and the bloodlust gleam on her face was the most evil thing I have even seen.

Mister Cunningham stormed back into the house, cleaned his riding crop, and went back to the store. Jim slipped his tied hands loose from the crossbar and shuffled back to his shed. Later, as soon as Miz Polly had gone to sleep, I sneaked down to the shed. I listened, then knocked.

"Come on in, Miss Lizzie, I know it's you. Did you get a whupping, too?" For once I wished I could say, "Yes," and felt ashamed that I couldn't.

"Jim, I've brought some buttermilk poultices like Aunt Maud used to put on my risin's. Maybe they will help." Jim was lying on his stomach, and as I began to daub his back with the poultice, he began crooning an old Negro spiritual that I hadn't never heard. I said, "You sure look funny, Jim, all black and red and white." He just kept on crooning after I had finished.

I said, "Jim, why don't you run away—go out to the Indian Territory and get you a place? Uncle Billy says that the Seminole Indians took their slaves with them from Florida, but they warn't treated bad—they even married them. I bet you could find some friends out there."

"Now, Miss Lizzie, what would Miz Polly do with me gone, and who would keep an eye on you? But when I get a whupping like today, I do think about it. I think about it a lot."

"If I was older, that's what I'd do. They would hunt for me, but I would fool them. Why, I'd wait till the south-bound freight to Little Rock came through, and I'd make sure they missed me about that time and think I was off to Little Rock, but I would lay low until the night freight came through heading west, and that's what I would catch. That's what you ought to do, Jim."

He didn't say no more, but put his face down on his hands and sighed. It was time for me to go to the store, so Miz Sally could come home and rest a bit, so I took off.

After cleaning up around the store, I headed home to get supper ready for Mister Cunningham. I went around to the back door, as was my habit ever since I found out that using the front door was a sure date with the razor strop. I wondered how Jim was doing, but didn't have time to check on him. Then I saw his hoe, with mine right beside it, leaning up again the clothesline post where he had got whipped.

By the time Mister Cunningham got home it was time, not only for supper, but to change Miz Polly's bedsheets again. Well, I couldn't do it by myself, so Mr. Cunningham hollered out the back door for Jim, and stopped in the middle of his holler when he saw the hoes. Striding down to the shed, he flung the door open, looked in, then starting running back to the house. "That nigger's gone! He's done gone and run off. Wait till I get my hands around his neck!"

I said, "Where do you reckon Jim went, Mister Cunningham?"

He whirled around on me like a shot, and said, "Don't you ever use that name again. He's not got no name, he's just a nigger, and I 'low he's done stole a bunch of stuff. I'm going to go get Haskins and we'll catch him. I helped that ungrateful nigger, fed him, took care of him, and look how he's treated me!"

He hitched the buggy by himself and went tearing off. Miz Sally had to help me with the bed and Miz Polly, a task she despised, or maybe it warn't the task as much as her sister. She didn't like her sister, and took few pains to hide it. Nor did she hide it from Mister Cunningham, because I had heard them at the store on several occasions, laughing and carrying on. I had almost stumbled in on them in the feed room late one rainy day when there were no customers around. From the noise I thought they must be moving the sacks of feed, but something told me not to make any noise, but to get out of there. Which I did, after listening for a little bit.

The buggy came flying back with Haskins and Mister Cunningham leaning over the dash. They stopped long enough to get some rope and a lantern, and ask me when I thought that nigger left. I studied for a minute, then said, "Yes sir, I think it was just a bit before the south-bound freight came through town, but he didn't have anything with him the last time I saw him."

"Shut up! You don't know anything about it. Niggers will steal you blind as soon as you turn your back. But he is going to larn his lesson." Then they took off again.

I laid on my bed until I heard the west-bound night freight whistle in the distance. Then I got up, went to the window, and waited as it slowed through town, then whistled again as it beat up speed for the run to the west. I said to myself with exultation, "Go, Jim, go!"

Mister Cunningham and Haskins got back a couple of days later, the worse for wear and being empty-handed, the horse slathered, and the buckboard in dire need of another paint job. As soon as I saw them I figured it was a good time to not be seen, because the need to take it out on someone stuck out all over them. I was sweeping the store when they drove up at the front, so I slipped out the back way and beat it home.

Miz Polly was hammering with her fly swatter, so I hollered, "Just a minute, I'm putting on the black-eyed peas to warm, I'll be there in a minute!" In a long minute, after I had got the fire going, and the cornbread started, I went to tend to her needs.

Happily, she hadn't fouled the bed, but she wanted to know, "Whar's my nigger? The backyard needs tending, and you're neglecting it. Whar's Mister Cunningham? I'll get you straightened out, you lazy brat."

As if they had been called, in came both my unfavorite gentlemen. I didn't say anything, but busied myself setting the table and pouring some buttermilk. The cornbread would soon be done, and the peas were hot, so I quartered some white onions and started back in the kitchen.

Haskins grabbed me by the elbow, and snarled, "I bet you know where that nigger is, don't you? Pussyfooting around here like little Miss Innocent. Like as not, you'll try to get out of here just like he did. Come over here and set down where I can see yore eyes when you answer me." He thrust me into one of the cane-bottomed dining chairs near the lamp. I thought, "Well, I'm finally getting to sit in the dining room. First thing you know, they'll want me to eat with them."

The front screen slammed, and Miz Sally came in from the store, took in the scene, and said, "What are you doing in my chair?"

Since she asked, I decided to answer, "Well, Haskins here don't want me to serve supper, so I guess it will be up to you, or we'll all do without. You should be able to find the cornbread, 'cause that smell you smell is it burning right now."

Haskins slammed his hand down on the table, and said, "You impertinent yokel! Get in thar and take care of this meal. Then you get right back in here and I'm gonna ask you some questions. You've got that conniving look on your face."

It was funny he should think that, since at that moment I really warn't conniving anything. But since he mentioned it, I got me an idea.

I retreated to the kitchen and got the cornbread, dumped it out of the skillet and scraped some of the black off the bottom. In the pocket of my dress I had a small bottle of rat poison that I'd picked up at the store earlier to take care of some varmints in the pantry. I set it on the cabinet in a place I had picked out, noticeable, but not too much. Then I poured up the peas, and delivered them to the table. I went back to the kitchen, where I banged around on a few pans, and lingered, waiting.

They must have been hungry, because it warn't long before Mister Cunningham hollered, "What's taking you so long? Git in this dining room with that cornbread and the onions!"

I dawdled a little longer, then here he came. "What are you doing in here? Git in here this minute!" I picked up the plate of cornbread and the onions and carried them into the dining room without meeting his eye. As I passed , I sensed, rather than saw, him looking around the kitchen, then I sorta saw a catch in his movements as he stopped dead in the water. He had seen my little bottle on the cabinet, and recognized it.

I stood back while Miz Sally and Haskins sat down, and then like a late arrival, Mister Cunningham came from the kitchen. He looked kinda pale around the gills, but I still didn't meet his eye directly. He asked Haskins to say grace, then he stood up and said, "Seeing as how Lizzie is here, and has worked so hard on this meal, I think she should be seated and eat with us."

Haskins and Miz Sally looked dumbfounded, but slightly relieved when I said, "No, sir, I don't think that would be fittin'. Besides, I ain't hungry."

Mister Cunningham said, "Hogwash! A growing kid like you, not hungry? I insist. In fact, we're gonna let you eat first, eat all you want, then we'll eat while you go do the last of the chores."

I sat down uncertainly, and said, "Do you think there will be enough peas, Mister Cunningham? Maybe I better leave those for you all, and I'll just eat cornbread and onion, and maybe drink some buttermilk later on." I looked at him hopefully.

He just smiled, and said, "Why, Lizzie, there's plenty of food, here, let me help yore plate." Well, he piled my plate with peas, pushed his own glass of buttermilk over to my place, and passed me the cornbread and onions. They watched while I ate, transfixed at the sight. I asked for some more cornbread, crumbled it into my buttermilk, and finished it off with my spoon. Finished, I said, "That was a fine meal. Now if you'll excuse me, I'll get about my chores, while you all eat."

Once in the kitchen, I grabbed my little bottle and dropped it out the window into the hydrangea bush where I could retrieve it later, and set about boiling water to wash the dishes. I heard no sound from the dining room except for a "Shhhh!" from Mister Cunningham. I smiled to myself, went to the screen door and slammed it, then stepped back into the kitchen to listen. I could hear Mister Cunningham hissing, "She's got a bottle of strychnine in the kitchen. Don't touch those peas!" Miz Sally yelped like a stepped-on hound, and Mister Cunningham shushed her up.

Haskins warn't too successful keeping his voice down, "Strychnine! She was going to poison us! But ... but she ate the peas right here before our eyes. What's going on here? We better get to the bottom of this. As soon as she comes back in the house, we are going to have a good little talk." I slammed the screen once more, and started busying myself around the stove.

They all three came into the kitchen, and stood there looking at me.

I asked, "You all through, already? There ain't no more in here. I told you if I ate, there wouldn't be enough."

Mister Cunningham's eyes were darting around the kitchen like fireflies on a summer night, looking, looking, but looking in vain. "What did you do with it, you little schemer, you?" Haskins and Miz Sally looked at him a little strangely, then at each other. Miz Sally shook her head, saying "I need a drink, but I think Mister Cunningham here has had one too many."

"Lizzie! Lizzie!" Miz Polly was calling from the back bedroom. "Whar is that worthless Lizzie? Whar is my nigger? Whar is everybody? I need new sheets!"

I looked at Miz Sally and said, "Haskins here wants to ask me some questions, so I guess you'll have to take care of yore sister this time."

She glared at me, then at Haskins, and said, "Let the kid be. She's got work to do."

CHAPTER FIFTEEN

I NEVER KNEW THAT JOSIE HAD SENT ME ANY LETTERS, UNTIL THE DAY when Miz Polly had a colic fit. With Jim no longer there to send to the store for help, I was stuck between a rock and a hard place. What to do? Leave her or stay with her? "There's some paregoric around here somewhere, look for it!" she gasped, pointing a shriveled finger. "Look in Sally's room!"

Well, I hadn't ever been in Miz Sally's room before, but felt like I had a good enough excuse. I found the paregoric, all right, plus some letters with my name on them. I hurriedly gave Miz Polly a dose, and she soon settled down and went to sleep.

I crept back into Miz Sally's room, and stood by the front window where I could see down the road to the store with half an eye, while I read the letters. Josie was living with William and his wife in a place near Horntown in the Indian Territory. One letter read in part, "... Lizzie, you got to come out here and be with your family. Enclosed is money for your train fare."

I put the letters back in the envelopes and stuck them back like I found them in the night stand with the paregoric. Money? I didn't see no money. Suddenly I wished that I could talk to someone I trusted—Aunt Hettie, or Kinsey, or even Judge Boudreau. What in the Sam Hill was I going to do? The water just kept getting deeper and deeper.

At supper that evening I set two places. Haskins had heard something about a Negro over in the Atkins jail, and had gone over to see if it was Jim. I was standing up in the kitchen eating some buttermilk and cornbread when I heard Miz Sally come in the front door. I heard her go to her room and after a little bit she went back to see how her sister was doing. I stood real still, not wanting to talk to her, when I heard Miz Polly say, "You would like for me to die, wouldn't you? Don't think I don't know about you and Mister Cunningham—I can read it on yore face. Well, I almost did die today. Worst colic fit I've ever had. I finally got that lazy Lizzie to find some paregoric in your room, and I'm probably going to live."

Miz Sally exploded, "You did what?" Then it sank in on me. I had put the paregoric right back where I had found it, but didn't think that I might as well have left a note saying, "Miz Sally, I have read those letters you didn't want me to know about."

"Lizzie, where are you? Come here this instant!" I had already set the milk glass down, and was easing out the back door, going around the side so Miz Polly wouldn't see me. I heard the front door slam, and peeking around the corner I saw Miz Sally almost in a trot heading for the store. I ran back in the house and filled a pillowcase with things that were mine, hurried outside again by the back door, and beat it south behind the row of cedars so I could head for the back door of the store.

I stopped to catch my breath, and saw Mister Cunningham and Miz Sally boring down the road for the house. Miz Sally was saying, "That wretched brat has been prowling in my room and she found those letters that came to her, I know she did!" Mister Cunningham cut her off, saying, "How could you be so stupid, leaving them around just inviting someone to read them?"

I made it to the back door of the store, hesitated, then tried the knob. Sure enough, they had been so excited that they forgot to lock the door. I knew they were combing the place for me at the house, so I didn't have time to waste.

I had a short conversation with God. "Lord, they stole my money. Is it wrong for me to steal what was stole from me?" While God was considering, I went to the cash register, got out the amount of money that Josie said in the letter William had included, plus a nickel for my allowance, and beat it back out the back door.

"Where to now?" I wondered. My advice to Jim had been to cut and run so that it looked like he was headed for Little Rock, then catch the westbound train. But that was a freight train, and I knew I couldn't hop one of those. Besides, it warn't dark yet, and if they didn't have their wits on backwards, they would know that I would head for the Indian Territory, and that place called Horntown.

I decided to climb the hill and wait in the cemetery till I figured out what to do. It was a good place to keep watch on the town, anyway. I might have some friends buried in that graveyard—I sure didn't know of any down in the town. I saw Mister Cunningham go down to the train station long about dark, so I knew that buying a ticket was out of the question; they'd nab me sure!

Well, I didn't have enough money to try for the Little Rock train and then double back to the west, and besides, I didn't know anyone in that direction. I gave some thought to burning down the store and getting on the train while everybody was fighting the fire, but then realized that they would catch me, and put me in jail, but not in the same jail with Uncle Billy since I was a kid and a girl, so I gave up on that idea. I thought about trying to get to Hot Springs to Judge Boudreau, until I remembered his "I'm sorry, Lizzie..."

It was about time for the passenger train running west, so I headed east and cut across the track, walked the trestle over the slough just east of town, then beat it through the bushes on the north side till I got opposite where I thought the caboose would be when the train stopped for passengers, mail, and water.

I could see Mister Cunningham and the station agent standing on the siding gesturing and talking. I couldn't hear from where I was, but it didn't take much imagination to know what they were saying. There warn't anyone at the station to get on, but it had to stop anyway.

It was a good guess; when the train pulled in I could see into all the windows as it crawled slowly by, and I could see that someone was walking down one of the aisles, getting ready to get off when the train stopped rolling. It was Haskins. I thought he was across the river at Atkins, looking for Jim, but I guess he was beating both sides of the bush. I saw him jump off the train, hesitate when he saw Mister Cunningham, then they hurried toward each other.

The train didn't stay stopped long. Just as it was pulling out, I pulled up on the rear of the caboose—barking my shins on the way up—eased through the door, and hunkered down below the window, half hidden behind some rain slickers hanging on a hook. I prayed. Then I looked back through the rear door at the rapidly disappearing station. Still silhouetted in the yellow light were Cunningham and Haskins. I saw Haskins throw his hat on the platform and stomp it, and thought I could see, but it was probably just my imagination, the outline of his ears jutting out from his head.

It was only a question of time. They knew that I hadn't got on the train because I didn't buy a ticket, and besides, they thought I didn't have any money. However, when either Miz Sally or Mister Cunningham got back to the store, they would count every nickel in that money box. Then they would know, and probably figure out what I had done.

Well, they could send a telegram to stop the train, but I'd be in the Indian Territory before morning. Or so I hoped. I looked around, saw that no one had noticed me get on. Everyone was facing forward, and not very many at that. I cautiously made my way up the aisle and sat down across the aisle from a sleeping man. I pretended to be asleep too when I heard the door open at the front of the car. It was the conductor, and he was coming back toward me. I opened one eye, and caught him looking right at my pillowcase.

"Young lady, when did you get on, and where is your ticket?" The man across the aisle woke up while I was considering my answer. "Well?" he prompted.

I said, "Sir, I didn't have time to buy a ticket, so I just got on at the caboose. I've got money here—my brother William said it would be just the right amount to get me to Horntown, wherever that is."

My neighbor across the aisle said, "Well, Conductor, it looks like we've got another 'Boomer' here. On her way to the Indian Territory to stake out a claim. Isn't that right, young lady?" He laughed, but it warn't unpleasant.

The conductor scratched his head and said, "Well, I'll take yore fare, but I'm going to have to take you on to Wewoka, so we can check out and see whether you're a runaway, or not. What did you say yore name was?"

I thought about that one, then bridled, "Well, if you think I'm a runaway, then you wouldn't believe me, whatever name I gave you. But I ain't ashamed of my name. I'm just a country girl, and my name is Lizzie Tackett!"

I stuck out the money—all of it except my nickel—and the conductor kind of grinned, and said, "Well, Miss Lizzie Tackett, you have just purchased a one-way fare to Wewoka. Make yourself comfortable."

We put on coal at Waldron, and took on a few passengers. Later, just before crossing out of Arkansas we made a water stop. By that time I had got acquainted with the man across the aisle, and he was teaching me checkers. I didn't bother to tell him that Uncle Billy and Aunt Maud had already taught me enough so that they wouldn't play me any more. Actually he didn't ask me if I could play, he just said, "Let me teach you the game of checkers, it's too noisy to sleep anyway."

I let him beat me several games, then I started playing him closer. I took a lot longer to study out moves than necessary, so he warn't suspicious. The conductor had come back to stand and watch us, leaning on the back of the seat. After a while he said, "Say, gent, let me play this here runaway young lady a game or two. Checkers is my weakness and I can't resist them."

My "teacher" said, "Waal, I guess that would be all right with me, but

I think you ought to make it interesting. Why don't you put yore money where yore tobacco is?"

"Shaw, she don't have money enough to make it interesting. Unless you want to risk some of your own by loaning it to her. How much did you have in mind?"

Mister Shaw said, "Waal, I think night rates should be higher than day rates ... how about five dollars?"

I stared at him, thought I saw him wink at me, but was so startled by the huge sum of five dollars, that I didn't say anything. Then I thought, "I haven't fooled this gentleman at all!" So I said to the conductor, "You're right, I don't have any money, nothing but a nickel. But I can't take money from a stranger ... but I tell you what I will do. If you win, and this gentleman wants to give you five dollars, that's all right with me. But if I win, then you have to let me off at Horntown, instead of this here Wewoka you're talking about."

The conductor said, "I couldn't do that, but it won't do any harm to play you, because you can't beat me anyway. Maybe I can teach you something."

Mister Shaw said, "Wait up now, a deal's a deal. You got to have a bet on both sides. As far as I'm concerned, my five dollars is laying here on the seat, waiting for you if you win, and this lady's get-off at Horntown is the bet on the other side. What's the matter, don't you think you can beat her?"

I gave up a couple of checkers early, then suckered him into a double-jump set-up, got a "king," and chased him down. He stared at me with a red face, then looked at my "teacher." "This is the best two out of three, right? That's the only way I play."

"Mister Conductor, you didn't say anything about three games," I protested. "I won that game fair and square. If you are going to stretch on me, then put some more up."

Mister Shaw cackled and said, "This little 'Boomer' has got you dead! What do you want to bet this time? And is it for Game Two, and another bet for Game Three, or will it be 'best three out of five'?" I felt sorry for the conductor with someone egging him like that, because I knew that flustered minds can't pitch worshers or play checkers neither. But I warn't sorry about winning. I never am.

We stopped at Wilburton and my "teacher" bought me breakfast. He said, "I reckon it will be all right with you for me to pay, seeing I 'taught' you so much about checkers, won't it?"

I sniffed and said, "I reckon so, or if you want, we can play a game to see who gets the bill. And by the way, why did you call me a 'Boomer'?"

He explained that a "Boomer" was someone who lined up waiting for the "Boom" of the cannon signaling time to rush off into the prairie ahead of someone else and drive a stake for a homestead. A "Sooner" was someone who illegally crossed the line during a land rush, often sneaking in during the night before the rush was to begin at dawn. I thought about Keithley, and wondered if he was headed for one of those land rushes when he left Hot Springs.

I got off at Horntown in the morning with a wave from my "teacher," and the fifteen dollars I won from the conductor burning in my pocket. I clutched my pillowcase, and looked all around. As the train pulled away, I made a note to look at the train number, thinking I had better not ride that one again.

Horntown warn't a large place, but it was sure full of folks when I got off. They were having some kind of celebration, combined with an Indian pow-wow, a snake-oil medicine show, an itinerant preacher holding forth about an arbor meeting that night, and various hawkers and salesmen.

While I was trying to decide which way to go, the crowd parted like a flock of scared guineas, as a bare-backed horse race thundered by in a cloud of dust and wild whoops. I jumped for the side of the narrow street, and climbed up on a pile of sacks of feed and sat on a barrel of nails. I could see over the crowd from there—maybe I would see my brother, William.

I had seen Indians before, back in Arkansas, but there they were usually very quiet, somber, and moving softly. Here they were in groups, pigtailed and many dressed out in their finery. I fingered my own pigtails as I watched them. Somewhere one of them was beating on a tomtom, and the cadence was making my feet jiggle.

Then I heard some excited, high-pitched palavering on the other side of the wagon parked next to the feed store where I was. Some folks were laying bets. I slid down and walked over to listen, but couldn't see who or what was going on, so I looked for another high perch. Nothing seemed to be available, so I grabbed the front wheel of the wagon, and climbed up into the seat, and stood up to look things over.

Then I thought I heard a voice I knew, just as one of the men saw me—it was Keithley, but he didn't let on he'd seen me, or that he knew me if he had. He finished what he was saying with, "…doubles it'll be. I'll even choose me a blind partner. Hey you," he said, pointing at me, "did you just get off that train from Wilburton?"

I said, "Yeah, I just got off the train, is there something wrong with that?"

Keithley said, "Come on down from up there, young lady, you're going to be my partner in this here doubles worshers game. These two jaspers here from Kansas claim they are world-beaters, and I'm going to take them down to size! What's yore name?"

I looked at him and the Kansas opponents, and I figured out his scheme. I said, "I don't know that it's any of your business, but I'm just a country girl from Arkansas, and my name is Lizzie Tackett. What's yourn?"

After Keithley introduced himself, and then the Kansas gentlemen, he explained "worshers" to me, saying that the object was to pitch underhanded and make the worshers go in the holes. He pointed about twenty feet away where there were three holes lined up in a row, straight as an arrow, and about twelve inches between each hole. He continued, "Lizzie, the nearest hole counts 'one,' the next hole counts 'three,' and the back hole counts 'five.' If a worsher lands in a hole on top of yore opponent's then you cancel each other. If you hang over the 'three' hole you score two, and if you hang over the 'five' hole you score four. If nobody makes a hole, or if 'holers' are cancelled out, then the nearest worsher is worth one point. Have you ever played this game before? Do you understand the rules?"

I said, "No" and "Yes" to his double-barreled questions, and asked if I could see those worshers. I asked, "How long do we play? I've got to look for my brother."

The Kansas team snorted, but my partner said, "Waal, I think we ought to play the best two out of three games of twenty-one. You reckon you can stay that long?"

I allowed as I might, but added, "I ain't et since breakfast, and I'm shore hungry." The Kansas team snorted again, and someone in the gathering crowd of onlookers yipped, and grabbed a passing Indian by the pigtail, and said, "Gottum fry bread? Papoose hungry. Fry bread? Dollar!" And so I was introduced to fry bread. Not as good as cornbread, but I warn't picky.

The first game began. I was kinda glad we were playing partners, because I was twenty feet from Keithley most of the time, and what I wanted in the worst way was to talk to him, and I didn't figure it would be very smart to give away that we knowed each other. The Kansas dude beside me kept over-explaining the rules to me, so I wouldn't go over the toe line, and so I wouldn't step sideways to get a clear shot at the back hole, just three feet each side of the centerline.

I looked at him and asked, "What do I get if we win?"

He slapped his leg, doubled over, coughed, then spit and said, "Well, normally if you're going to play this game, you put up some money, but I reckon you don't have any, do you?" I asked, "You mean I bet agin you and you bet agin me? I thought we were playing doubles."

He said, "Shore we are, and the winners get the pot to split. But what I'm talking to you about is a little side bet, just between you and me. Like a game within a game."

I hollered down to my partner, "Is that right, Mister? Do I play agin this here jasper, too? And if I beat him, does he owe me the side bet, or is that part of the pot?" I wanted to nail that down, because I had the feeling this jasper was going to weasel out of turning loose of any of his money.

Keithley answered, "Have you got any money, Lizzie?"

"I got fifteen dollars."

Keithley said, "Well, Mister Jayhawker, I think she's calling you. What are you going to do?" Then turning to the crowd, Keithley said, "Gentlemen, is there anyone who would like to sweeten the kitty? This little lady is full enough of spunk to lay her own money agin this Jayhawker, but that don't leave her none for the pot. How about a little help?" The crowd was having fun, so they raised a hat of cash, which when counted came to twenty dollars. Keithley said, "Waal, here's my twenty. Now that means these here Northerners have to put twenty dollars each into the pot."

It seemed like it was getting warmer, with those Kansas jaspers rubbing their hands in anticipation. They gave me first shot, but I declined, saying I didn't know for sure how to shoot at three holes at once, so I'd rather follow. My opponent, who said his name was Hiram, lofted his first shot in front of the "one" hole, and it went in. He followed with a harder shot, to the "three" hole, I suppose. You couldn't be sure because it warn't close enough to even guess.

I asked Hiram, "Did you make what you was aiming at?"

He scowled and said, "Shut up and pitch!" I slid one by the "one" hole and it tipped into the "three" hole. "Lucky shot!" said Hiram, "but we're still three to one."

I said, "No sir, we ain't," and let fly to cover his "one." I looked around and inspected the crowd while Keithley and his opponent, Troy, pitched. I figured Keithley would have no problem. I was going to concentrate on doing my part of the damage. I had to pitch first since I scored, so I decided to experiment a little. I threw an "air" for the "three" hole. If I made it, fine, and if not, then I probably would slide into the "five" hole. It hit the back edge of the "three" hole, and fell back in. My next shot I slid in from the left side, straight into the "five" hole. The crowd yelled in unison, and I could see new bets being placed, and looks of panic on some faces.

Hiram asked suspiciously, "Are you sure you've never played this game?"

I said, truthfully, "I never saw three holes lined up like that in my life." While the other end pitched back, I thought, "Hey, I think I like this layout about as well as the Yell County layout." It took a different kind of finesse, and the strategy changed.

Hiram downed a "three," but that was all. By that time Keithley had ten points to go with my eight, and Troy had added three points to Hiram's none. We were ahead eighteen to three.

I decided to work in a little change of pace. Since I was leading off again, and it looked like I would be for the rest of the game, I tried laying my worshers in front of the holes. That would force Hiram to nudge mine in accidentally, or else shoot wide and wild. I put my first one in front of the "one" hole, and laid my second worsher in front of the "three" hole, actually a "hanger." Hiram said something under his breath that must not have tasted good, because he scowled and spat halfway to the target.

I said, "Hiram, you're almost as good spittin' as you are with worshers." He didn't say nothing, but just looked at his work ahead.

After that round, in which Hiram got a roller "five," and nudged my worsher into the "one" hole with his on top, we were setting at eighteen to eight. Keithley chortled, offered Troy one of his worshers, then sank his loner in the "three" hole to set up the challenge for Troy. He could have tried for two "fives" and a "three," which would have left us tied eighteen to eighteen. Or he could at least cancel Keithley's "three" and stave off the game ending on that round. He tried all three worshers, trying to cover Keithley's, and missed them all.

I had first pitch in Game Two. I decided to try to burn the bridges. I slid my first worsher in from the left side, and my second from the right side, both in the "five" hole. The crowd had got quiet. Hiram said, "You bitch," under his breath, but I think Keithley heard him, because I could see his eyes harden from twenty-six feet away.

I said, like I didn't understand him, "I've already pitched, it's your pitch." Someone in the crowd near our end tittered. Hiram hung a leaner, but it didn't count. His other worsher might as well have been hung around his neck.

Keithley held his worshers up like he was aiming at Hiram through the holes, and threw two "airs," both into the "five" hole. He said, "That's for yore language, Hiram!" Troy threw his worshers down on the ground, and stomped around, then thinking better of that forty dollars, he came back and picked them up. In that frame of mind you can't hit nothing. He hit nothing, and suddenly we were sitting at twenty to nothing.

I asked Hiram if he knew any other games, because I had expected this to last longer, and besides, I didn't see my brother, William, anywhere. He said, "Pitch, and get it over with. I need a drink!"

I said, "You mean you ain't a-gonna throw?"

Hiram said, "No, I ain't a-gonna throw. I ain't going to let no Arkansas pup outpitch me. I quit!" He stalked off in search of a drink. His partner stood staring after him, open-mouthed. He did have the decency to come down and meet me. He looked me in the eye, sizing me up, and said, "Hmmm! A country girl, huh. I've been taken before, but not this neat and sweet." Then he laughed, "A country girl? I need a drink!"

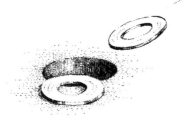

CHAPTER SIXTEEN

KEITHLEY AND I COUNTED OUR MONEY, AND I ASKED HIM IF THERE WAS somewhere we could go so I could talk to him. He said, "Yep, I know just the place. I've got a friend who's opened a pie shop for this festival. She's making more money than anyone here. She'll bed you down tonight, if you don't see William first. Let's go there and talk in her kitchen, and maybe get to taste some of her creations."

Imogine was a tall, pretty gal who looked like she might be full-blood Indian but talked English as plain as he did. Keithley sat me down in the back of the kitchen in her little frame house right on the main street, and I brought him up to date on all that had happened since the trial. He didn't say anything while I talked, but I could see his jaw muscles working.

When I was all through, he said, "Well, let's tackle this one thing at a time. Tell me what this Jim looks like. You don't need to tell me what Haskins and Cunningham look like—I saw them at the trial. I would like to see them one more time, but I guess that can wait." I described Jim, and told him about what Uncle Billy had said about the Seminole Indians. Keithley looked up and said, "That's right. If there is anywhere in this country that he will be accepted for his own worth, it would be there. Wewoka is the capitol of the Seminole Nation, or at least it is now, since the Government moved as many as they could catch in Florida out here. That conductor was going to put you out there, remember? I may just go up that-a-way and see if anyone there has heard of this Jim."

I thought Keithley sounded a little bitter talking about the Seminoles, so I asked him if he was part Seminole. He said, "No, Lizzie, I'm mostly Muskogee, or Creek if you like, but in the old days our tribe was neighbor to the Seminole, and we even had a friendly war going between us. Then the white man came, thought an Indian was an Indian, so they started herding us west. Now this whole Indian Territory is filled with dozens of tribes, only a few of which can really call this home."

I lay awake that night thinking how nice it would be to know who you were, regardless of which tribe you came from, or if you were white, which country. And to know where your grandfathers had come from. Keithley, or even Jim, might be bitter and they had a right to be, but at least they had some history—I had only one page in my Tackett book. Well, so I was an orphan, but at least I was in the Bible, as Aunt Hettie once said.

Keithley didn't waste any time; when I got up next morning, he was already gone to Wewoka. I was fretting about how to locate William, but Imogine said to wait till Keithley got back, and she would see that he took me to the Tackett place.

"In the meantime," she said, "why don't you help me keep turning these pies out?" I was glad to have something to occupy my mind, so I turned to. Aunt Maud had already taught me a little about pies, but I learned a lot more. First off, I fell in love with her "Fly Pie," as she called it. It was made with vinegar, some nuts, butter, sugar, and spices, and a smidgen of salt. Imogine used a flaky crust laid out like a cobbler, though she said that it was just as good made out of leftover biscuits.

I was curious and asked her why it was called "Fly Pie." She said, "Why, Hon, see that tea towel I've got spread over that dishpan over there? It's full of vinegar cobbler—and if I didn't have the tea towel over it, the flies wouldn't be able to fly across that pan without falling in. Take a sniff and you'll see what I mean." I would say a strong sniff of that pan ran a close second to Uncle Billy's squeezings. But that pie is some good, especially with a little cream poured over it.

I really wanted to get out and see what all was going on, but Imogine kept me busy. Actually I was good for business, because we had a lot of customers who came by just to see "that country girl from Arkansas who shore knows how to pitch worshers."

That evening, when business cooled down, Imogine took me out for a walk. Lanterns were plentiful up and down the street, and at the far end there was this big brush arbor where the itinerant preacher I had heard on my arrival was holding a revival meeting. Imogine called it a "protracted" meeting. I liked singing, but could do without a lot of the thumping, stomping, and yelling that I associated with preachers. When we got closer, we could see a couple of old codgers up front playing on handsaws with fiddle bows. The music they made was pretty, in a peculiar sort of way, but the camp dogs kept interrupting with a mournful howling when they hit some of the higher notes. There warn't any seats left, if you could call them seats—kegs, buckets, and scantlings resting on sawhorses was all there was to sit on. Imogine and me, we just stood at the back and listened.

After the music, the preacher got up to declare the Word. I was already tired and a little sleepy, wishing for a good pallet on the ground, when something woke me up good and proper. That preacher sure sounded familiar, and he sure looked familiar, but I couldn't place him. I stared at him, and as I listened, I had a vision bubble up out of the depths of my memory of a pale, lanky man rising buck-naked up out of a storm cellar with a jug on his shoulder. It looked like everyone in Arkansas had decided to come to the Indian Territory. It was my neighbor of old—Mister Robbins! I hadn't forgotten him, not by a long shot. I had just been too busy recently with Haskins and Cunningham to give him much thought...except in my worst nightmares. "So this is where you went off to after you went and kilt Miz Robbins," I said under my breath.

I slipped away from Imogine without her noticing it, and circled around to the back of the arbor. It was mighty dark out of the lantern light of the brush arbor, but I soon got my night eyes, and saw the evangelist's covered wagon and rope corral set back near the creek that ran through town. I was pretty sure he wouldn't have a dog, since I remembered him kicking his late wife's hound around back on the farm, and finally knocking it in the head for barking at night. So I moved back to the wagon thinking I would be safe as long as I could hear him preaching. I stood there scheming, and listening to Mister Robbins in the distance calling for sinners to come to the loving arms of Jesus.

Exploring under the wagon seat, tucked under some horse blankets, I found two fruit jars. One was full, and the other had about a third gone. I unscrewed one of the Mason lids, verified with a sniff my suspicions that this warn't communion juice, and carried them down near the creek. There I poured them out, set one jar afloat in the stream, and skewered the other down in the sand. I gathered me up a couple of likely rocks, but it took only one tap to knock the head off the jar. Satisfied with my work, I took the lower half of the jar with its jagged edges back to the wagon, and set it on the wagon seat. Then I moseyed back to the gathering at the brush arbor.

I was back at Imogine's side when she said, "Where have you been? Looking for an outhouse, I suspect. Come on, let's go turn in, we'll have a busy day tomorrow. Keithley should be back by noon, and I'm going to let you make him a pie all by yourself."

There was no way I was going to sleep, not right away. I lay on my pallet in the kitchen and listened to the gospel meeting winding down. I got up and looked down the street, watching as one by one the lanterns were doused. People were shuffling back to their homes and campsites, getting ready for another day. In the distance I could see Mister Robbins with his lantern, making his way back to his wagon. I tiptoed outside and climbed up on the feed sacks I had used when I first arrived. There I sat, still as a rock, listening. Through the trees between the arbor and the creek I could see the lantern snuffed out, then silence prevailed. I could envision him scrabbling around under that horse blanket for the fruit jars slowly, then more insistently, then with a furious digging. I heard the squeak of the springs as he mounted up on to the seat, preparatory to crawling over for a thorough search. At that moment he must have sat down, because I heard a loud and agonized yell, followed by a flood of pleas upon the Almighty for swift and certain justice.

A couple of late stragglers were walking close by me, and I heard one say, "That is some preacher! Listen to him! The meeting is over, but he's back at his wagon, prevailing in prayer for the sins of the people."

I slept good that night. My conniving mind had an idea for tomorrow, but I would need Keithley to help me.

Imogine and I spent the next morning baking pies, and were ready for the evening onslaught of hungry men. We had cleaned up and were peeling our eyes for signs of Keithley. We were into the hot part of the afternoon, that time when the cicadas are at their loudest, and the hound dogs were moving to a new shady spot, looking for some cool dirt. I heard the clang of a horseshoe hitting the stob down under the cottonwoods by the creek, which made me cast a tentative eye at the nearest worsher pitching pit. Nobody was moving on the street.

I looked in the direction of the brush arbor, but didn't even consider going near that end of the street. I warn't quite sure what I would do if Mister Robbins took a hankering for pie, but there was always the kitchen to hide in.

Then I saw the dust cloud in the west, and two horses making their way into town. I shaded my eyes with my hand to squint at them, and then jumped down to run in and tell Imogine that Keithley was coming, and had someone else with him. Since they were coming from the end of town near the arbor, I didn't run to meet them, even though I wanted to. As they drew nearer I saw that the other rider was a black man wearing a dark uniform and broad-brimmed hat, and decked out with a shooting iron and a coiled blacksnake whip on the pommel of his saddle. When I first saw it was a Negro, my heart leaped, hoping Keithley had found Jim; but no, this was some kind of soldier.

They cut around the feed store to the horse lot, and I ran out to meet them. It *was* Jim! Dressed up in that fancy gear, and sitting in the saddle straight as a ramrod. He said, "Hello, Miz Lizzie, I'm shore glad to see you."

I studied him with a critical eye, and acted real serious-like, when I was actually so glad to see him I could have cut a buck-and-wing right there on the street. I just sniffed and said, "Well, Jim, I see you took my advice about how to get out here." Then I busted out laughing and said, "You should have seen old Haskins and Mister Cunningham tearing around the country in the buggy looking for you. You would have thought you belonged to them, the way they carried on. And Miz Polly, she kept crying, 'Whar's my nigger? Whar's my nigger?' But tell me where you got those clothes you're wearing. What kinda army are you in?"

Jim was smiling bigger than the brim of his hat as he said, "Miz Lizzie, it took me a while, but I got out to a place called Wewoka, which is where the Seminole Nation is located. That's whar I was taken in by them Indians and treated like family. You'll be surprised to know that yore doctoring skill was what got me this uniform."

Keithley interrupted and said, "Lizzie, why don't you let him get down off his horse before he grows to it? Any man talks better over a slab of pie, don't you know?"

I blushed and said, "I'm sorry, Keithley, but I just got carried away, and I'm busting to tell you all something, too. If you want chocolate pie, I'll get you some buttermilk to go with it, Jim, but Keithley here is going to get a surprise—I made him a vinegar pie!" I figured before it was over with, they both would eat both kinds.

We sat in the kitchen, the four of us including Imogine, and I said, "Jim, go ahead and tell me what you meant about my doctoring."

Jim said, "Lizzie, you remember after I got that whupping at the clothesline? You came down and put a buttermilk poultice on my back. Well, I was in Wewoka, east of town in the Seminole camp, when one of the men came in looking like he had a serious problem. I listened to him talking in their Seminole language, and I didn't understand anything, of course. Then the chief, I reckon that's who he was, turned to me and said, 'You know white man's medicine?' If he hadn't been so serious I would've laughed—asking a nigger if he knew 'white man's medicine.' How come he didn't ask me if I knew 'black man's medicine'? Well, they kinda drug me off to where this man lived, and there inside, stretched on a pallet was a young girl about yore age, and she had a cord tied around each ankle and each wrist, and the cords tied to stakes. That skeered me, but then I saw that she was covered with risin's, and they were trying to keep her from scratching them. She looked plumb pitiful. The chief asked me again, 'You know white man's medicine?'

"I remembered what you tole me that day, just like I remember everything you ever said, Miz Lizzie, and I tried to describe buttermilk to those pore people. You would have thought I was an Indian the way I drew pictures in the air, and tried to act out milking a cow. They must've thought I was trying to do a dance to drive out the evil spirits, but one squaw was looking in and it dawned on her what I was trying to say. It turned out she had worked for a white family, and one of her chores was churning. She started chattering at the men, and since I didn't know what to say, I just nodded my head over and over. Well, I don't know where they found it, but before long one of the men was back with a gourd of buttermilk. I tore off a piece of my shirt tail, and started daubing that buttermilk on that pore girl's risin's. I knew how they hurt, because I've had 'em myself, so I was real gentle. After watching me a while, the squaw—I guess it was her mama—moved up close, and I handed the gourd to her and motioned for her to tend to all the other risin's.

"I was ready to go back, but the chief let me know that I was to stay there in their camp. He give me a place to sleep, and, you'll like this one, Lizzie, showed me a pot of stew that they keep ready day and night by the front of their house or tent with some fry bread. I didn't dare ask what was in that stew, because I already thought I knew. Well, to shorten my story, the girl stopped moaning, and they untied her hands and feet. Next morning those risin's had gathered and come to a head. I showed the squaw how to hold a sharp knife over the fire, then cool the blade, and prick each of those sores. It was a blessed relief to that pore girl. I then showed her how to keep putting the buttermilk on the healing sores to draw out the rest of the pus.

"The men sat around outside the rest of the day, and I didn't have anything else to do, so I sat with them. I couldn't tell if any of them worked, or if the women did the work—in fact, I didn't see any work being done. Toward evening a group of uniformed men came to see the chief, and they palavered for a long time, then left. I made like I was asking, 'Who was that?' The reason I was interested, and a little nervous, was that they had guns and some were carrying whips. Their whips would put Mister Cunningham's to shame.

"We went down to the creek to wash off and get cool before turning in for the night. I went back to the camp with my shirt off, since I was all wet, and in the light of the lantern they saw my back. You know what it looks like, Miz Lizzie. I ain't ashamed of my whuppings or the scars, because I didn't deserve them, but I didn't think they was things to be proud of. Those Indians did. They jabbered around me for a long time before we went to bed. The next day the chief approached me and invited me to sit down and talk. It took almost till noon to get that conversation over with, because I didn't think I understood what he meant. After about the third time it was plain that he wanted me to be like the uniformed men I had seen the day before. He said I was going to be a 'Lighthorseman,' and carry a 'billy' stick and a whip and wear their uniform.

"They took me to this big old tree there on a gentle hillside, and told me to sit down and wait. Long about the middle of the afternoon, I saw a group of the uniformed Lighthorsemen come riding up with a trussed-up prisoner. They tied him to this 'Whupping Tree' and gave him what for. The chief said to me, 'You big arm. You whup.' So that's how I come to have these clothes, Lizzie. I'm one of the official Twenty Lighthorsemen now, thanks to yore teaching me how to doctor."

I realized that my mouth had been open a long time, and that Keithley was looking at me with amusement. I clapped it shut and sniffed, "I got someone I'd like for you to whip, Jim, but he's not an Indian." Turning to Keithley I said, "The Fruit Jar Man is in town."

Keithley asked, "What shenanigans have you gotten into now, Lizzie?

What do you mean, 'Fruit Jar Man'?"

I told the story about Miz Robbins, the storm cellar, and losing my best friend because of a broken fruit jar stuck in her windpipe. "He's here in this town, Keithley, and we can't touch him—he's the preacher in the brush arbor down the street." Then I told them about last night's trip down to Mister Robbins' wagon during the preaching time.

"So that's where you went , you little scamp!" exclaimed Imogine. "What if he had caught you?" Then she laughed, "So that's why that preacher is limping around today with a sore behind. I wonder if he got all the glass out!"

I replied, "I warn't in no danger. I could hear him plain, thundering and stomping back at the arbor. But I do have something that will take a little more doing, and if that pie was any good, you could help me."

Keithley said, "Now Lizzie, is there any such thing as a 'bad' pie? But truly, I'm not surprised that you can cook, though I imagine Imogine here has polished your skills a little bit. That pie was delicious, both of them! So I guess I surrender—what is it you want me to do?"

I already had it ready, so I went to my pallet and took out a wagon tail-gate plank that I had found in a junk pile at the wagon yard. "I want you to put this on Mister Robbins' wagon tonight."

Keithley looked puzzled, saying, "Don't he have a tail gate already, Lizzie, and what for would you be wanting to give him anything?" Then he saw what I had done to the plank, turned it around to read, chuckled, and said, "At yore service, Ma'am. You say when and I'll see that it gets done."

The preacher left a couple of lanterns burning at his campsite that night during the services. Maybe some folks thought that was kinda strange, but I knew what he was doing; he didn't want any more snoopers around his wagon. It was the last night, and he had announced he was moving on to Dustin the next morning to hold a meeting there. He had just about milked the cow dry around Horntown.

According to the custom, the people who came to the meeting that night had brought some of this and some of that as a going-away present for the preacher—a "pounding," they called it. Keithley had managed to get my board into the arbor, where it served as a seat, but with the interesting side down. After the meeting, Keithley helped load the various fruits of the "pounding" onto that board and got someone to help him carry it to the wagon. They took the tail-gate off the wagon and loaded everything into the back. Then Keithley switched my tail-gate for Mister Robbins', and closed the flap. Having worked the switch, he came back to the arbor with Robbins' tail-gate and laid it on two kegs for a bench. Mister Robbins was still waiting at the front, talking to some folks, and seeing if anyone else would decide at the last minute to make another offering.

Next morning, bright and early, Robbins hitched up his team to the wagon, looked carefully at the wagon seat, settled onto it gently, and said "Giddy-up." He swung through town, waving at whoever was out, of which there were quite a few. About halfway through town, he heard someone laugh, and turning around he saw a youth pointing at his wagon. Someone else laughed, and Robbins jerked on the reins. Tying them off on the brake handle, he eased himself off the seat and walked around to the back of the wagon. There, for all to see, were the words I had burned into the tail gate with a hot poker: *The Fruit Jar Man.*

I was watching through a crack in the curtains of the pie shop, and I could see several emotions sweep across his face: surprise, anger, suspicion, and fear. He probably had thought that the disappearance of his moonshine jars was the work of pranksters or some drunk in the town, but now he was making the association. Someone knew something about him. Did they know about his whiskey? Or was it that they knew about his 'fruit jar ragings' that had got him committed to the Little Rock asylum? Or did someone know or suspect that he had something to do with his wife's death?

He hurriedly got back in the wagon, slapped the reins and beat it out of town, looking back once. I turned to Keithley and Jim, who were in the pie shop, standing behind me, and said, "Well, what do you think? I know he killed his wife, but I can't prove it!"

Keithley had been as tickled as anyone about my fixing Mister Robbins' wagon, but then a dark brown study seemed to settle on his face.

"Lizzie, sit down over here and tell me again what all you can remember about Uncle Billy, everything that happened, and everything that took place in that courtroom," he said. "Remember that I left right after our worsher game. I've got a special reason for wanting to hear the story."

Puzzled, I began at the beginning and ended with my train ride to Horntown. When I finished, Keithley said, "I think we need to take a trip to Dustin; I hear there is going to be a protracted meeting over there, and we might oughta go."

I was mystified. I also didn't want to go. Sooner or later, Robbins was going to see me, probably recognize me, and then, like as not, I would have to strike out again for somewhere else. Besides, I wanted to see William and Josie, and anyone else of my family that was living out here. I told him so, and Keithley said, "Well, that's reasonable. As a matter of fact, I'd like to see some more of the family tree that you got whittled out of, myself. We'll go look them up tomorrow on our way to Dustin. I suspect they're farming down toward the South Canadian River bottoms, and I know someone at Lamar who can tell us if your folks live anywhere around there."

After breakfast the next day, Jim started back to Wewoka, and Imogine waved Keithley and me off, saying, "Don't forget where the pie is, and Keithley, don't you let anything happen to my new cook!"

We rode eastward, through the sand hills, then down over the ridge into the bottom lands. It was hot, dusty, and dry—but beautiful. I was surprised that the Government would be willing to give it to the Indians, but maybe they didn't know what they gave away. When I mentioned it to Keithley, he said, "No problem. If the government decides they made a mistake, they'll just throw away the treaty, and rewrite their history books again. They'll get the land if they want it."

We went down an erosion gully, found a wagon trail, and followed it to a homestead. There we asked for the whereabouts of the Tackett place, and the gaunt farmer in the barnyard pointed to the north and back west a bit. "You overshot it back there," he said. "I'm gonna bust up this sod next spring, and raise watermelons and cotton, but Tackett said he wants to try peanuts up there in the sand hills. That's where you'll find him."

When I heard the farmer say "Tackett," I knew he meant my brother William, and I got plumb excited. As we rode back over our trail, I jabbered on about William and Josie and my other brothers like it hadn't been nearly five years since I had seen any of them.

Keithley said, "Lizzie, I know you're looking forward to this reunion, and will probably want to stay with your folks, but first I've got to tell you something that might change your mind. You remember when I helped load the 'pounding' on top of your board, and got someone to help me carry it to the back of the preacher's wagon? Well, I had to scoot some things out of the way to make room for his 'haul,' and when I did I knocked the lid off of a shoebox setting on the wagonbed under some old rags and a scattering of hay. I'm not a natural prowler, but I uncovered some interesting items."

I stopped my horse, and gave him my full attention. "What items, Keithley?"

"Waal, I wanted to bring them and show you, but something told me I would be better off to leave them be for the time being. I'll just tell you what they are, and you tell me what you think. The first item was a butcher knife. 'Course that don't mean nothing by itself, but this one was dirty—still had blood, hair, and leaves stuck to it. Anyone that don't clean up their knife out in this country is kinda crazy, in my opinion. Don't you think so, Lizzie?"

Now I've got an excitable mind, even a conniving mind, but I didn't make the connection right away. I thought of how blood pretty nearly ruins a knife if you don't wash it off, and I thought of watching at hog-killing time, how a knife could get messed up. But what was Robbins doing with a hog-killing knife, with the nearest frost and hog-killing time being some seven months ago?

Keithley continued, "Lizzie, not only did I see that butcher knife while pushing his junk out of the way, but I stuck myself on a blamed piece of wire. Now every wagon has got some wire on it somewhere, or it ain't a wagon. But this wire was sorta wound around and around, like it had been used to tie around a fence post. Does that give you any ideas, Lizzie?"

Then it hit me. Robbins warn't no fruit jar man! Or he warn't *just* a fruit jar man: He was also a baling wire man. I sat on the horse, stunned, my mind reeling, trying to piece together what this meant for me, for pore old dead Miz Robbins, for Uncle Billy and Aunt Hettie.

"I see what you mean, Keithley. I reckon you're right, we need to make a trip to Dustin. Mister Robbins needs to be taught how to take better care of a butcher knife."

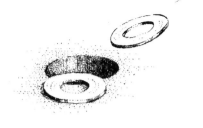

CHAPTER SEVENTEEN

EITHLEY AND I CAME OVER A RISE, AND WE COULD SEE A HOUSE AHEAD on a barren hill. There was a barn, and a couple of trees in the front yard. I could see the outhouse down the slope, and a well on the other side of the house. As we got closer, someone came out of the barn and stood leaning on a pitchfork, watching our approach. Then on the porch I saw somebody familiar. I quirted my horse and started galloping toward the house, and two more people came out of the house and they all started running to meet me. I could hear William whooping, and Josie screeching. That scared my horse and he stopped short, but I didn't. I went right over his head and landed in the dirt.

Suddenly my family was all over me, rolling and cavorting in that sandy red soil. "Air ye hurt, Lizzie? Air ye hurt?" I could've had a couple of broken legs and it wouldn't have mattered. I was among my kin! I looked at them all—William, his wife Annie, Jake, Patrick, and Josie. Josie was blubbering, "You did get my letters, you did get the money William sent!"

I looked at her and said, "Yeah, I got them, all right, but not the way you figured." Then I looked up as the shadow of a horse and rider fell over us. Keithley had gathered my mount, and had made a leisurely approach. I introduced him to all my folks, then we walked to the house. Patrick took the horses to the barn for water, and took off their saddles.

Later, sitting around the table eating hominy and gravy, with some squirrels that Jake had got that morning, we traded stories. They all, Josie in particular, kept gushing about we warn't never gonna get separated again. I stood up to stretch out the kinks of my ride and sudden dismount, went to the open front door and stepped out onto the porch. Josie and I walked around the yard, arm in arm, talking and letting me explore the place. It seemed like Josie was getting happier and happier, and I was getting sadder and sadder. We stopped under the tree by the well, and I said, "Josie, I'm afraid I can't stay long, at least not for now." I looked out across the landscape to the east and let my gaze sweep southward to where the mountains, purple in the distance, were lying like sleeping dogs, all pointed towards the river bottom.

"Josie, I think I'd like to come back here, but first there's some things that Keithley and I have to do, and I guess I'll have to go back to Arkansas for a little while. Keithley says that we need to tie up some loose ends ... probably with baling wire."

She looked at me curious-like, but I didn't try to explain anything until I could find out more myself.

Before we left the next morning I took a walk with each one of my kin. I didn't have a lot to say to William; it was just a comfort walking beside him, with him tugging at my pigtails from time to time, just like he'd done in happier times when we were younger. With Jake I talked about the mountains to the east, wondering if he would maybe take me there when I got back, all the way to the River to do some fishing or hunting. He said, "I've got a gun, Lizzie, but you won't need one—there's plenty of rocks for chunking, and there's plenty of things to chunk at." Patrick wanted to walk farther than the others. In fact, he said that he wished we could just keep walking and never look back. I said, "Patrick, I know you're still terribly upset about us losing Ma and Pa and the home place in Arkansas, but I aim to see about some things there, and if they work out right, you can go back there close to the old home place. How would you like that?" Maybe I fibbed a little bit, but I could read the hurt and lostness in Patrick's eyes, and wanted to promise him something, even if it didn't work out. I hoped against hope that somehow Uncle Billy could get out of prison and Patrick could live with him and Aunt Hettie awhile, where he could find the same kind of comfort they gave me. I didn't have any feeling about what was going to happen to me, but I knew that square in my path was Dustin, and maybe Arkansas again.

Keithley and I rode east down into the bottoms to take the road to Dustin, stopping at Lamar, so Keithley could send a telegram to Kinsey in Little Rock. I read what Keithley wrote and handed to the man. It said, *DUSTIN STOP BALING WIRE MAN STOP.* Keithley had to explain what the word *STOP* was for. Since we didn't know Kinsey's address, and had sent it to the Federal Building, Keithley said we would just stay around until we got a reply saying he had got our wire. We sent the telegram from the train station, and I was particularly entranced to see how a bunch of clickety-clacks made with a "key," as the man called it, could send words from here all the way to Little Rock. I pestered him to show me how to do it, and he let me play with one in the office that warn't hooked up.

It was getting towards the shank of the afternoon and we hadn't got a reply, so Keithley suggested that we go spend the night with some of his kin living down close to the River, and come back the next day to see if we had an answer. Cutting down into the bottom, we passed by many Indian families living in huts, some in houses, a few in tents or tepees, and a few white families living in more substantial houses mixed in.

On almost every hilltop, sometimes surrounded by plowed ground, we would see an Indian grave, with a low roof over it. They looked like dog houses that had sunk in until there was only a few inches between the edges of the roof and the ground. Keithley told me that white men were buried in boxes to keep the water out, but any fool should know that boxes ran out of air. Indians were buried in warm blankets, and the roof was to keep the rain out of their faces. Made sense to me. He showed me where food was left under the edge of the roof for the dead. I guess in a tight one could crawl under the gable end and get in out of the rain, but after seeing a dead rattlesnake in the road that someone had killed, I decided I would rather get wet. Keithley said that we were in big snake country, and to look sharp, and particularly be careful about the horse shying and throwing me on top of a waiting snake.

We got to the camp where his kin lived about two hours before sunset, and all the little kids surrounded us, eager to see Keithley and who the stranger was that he had with him. The women came out and shooed the children away, a young boy took our horses to a pole barn, and we were invited to sit. Well, not sit, exactly, but to hunker. Since Aunt Hettie had told me it was unladylike for girls to hunker, I stood up, and wandered around. I looked with approval on the abundant worsher pits, thinking that this was a nice place, snakes or no snakes. The huge trees, cicadas singing, nobody working up a sweat, and the river nearby were all somehow familiar to me. I missed Uncle Billy and Aunt Hettie, but I felt a deep stirring like I was among my own. It was confusing because "my own" were back up at Horntown, not here. Well, I thought, maybe instead of being part Indian, or part white, maybe I could just be all of both. Why not?

Keithley said that in order to spend the night I had to meet the grandfathers, who were hunkered under a white oak tree, smoking and talking. I was prepared to shake hands, or curtsy, or whatever a girl was supposed to do when formally introduced to Indians. Keithley told me to sit cross-legged, and he hunkered.

Then he began to talk in Indian to the old men. I saw them rivet their eyes on me, look at Keithley, occasionally chuckle, then look back at me. One of the younger of the men got up and walked around me, looking at me from different angles. I saw brief clouds of anger float across their faces at something that Keithley was saying, then they all laughed and slapped their thighs at something else. He must have told them my whole life history, or else it takes a long time to tell something in Indian.

Finally the oldest one of them got up and motioned me to stand. He took off a thong from around his wrist, which had a small leather bag attached to it. He lifted it to the sky, then let each of the men blow smoke on it, finally presenting it to me. He made some motions over my head like he was aiming at mosquitoes, and said something in Indian.

I looked up at Keithley and whispered, "What did he say then?"

Keithley smiled, and said, "He just gave you a name. He said that you may have a name that white folks gave you, but he had a better one. It's *CvtoceEnke*. It means 'Rockhand' ... and it also means that he is accepting you as a true Creek."

I couldn't think of anything better to do, so I reached in my pocket and got the smoky quartz that I had given to Uncle Billy, which he had given back to me, and knowing that Uncle Billy would approve, I gave it to the old chief. I thought about blowing smoke over it first, but I didn't have no smoke, so I spit on it and polished it a bit before handing it to the chief.

He held it up to the dying evening light, passed it around to the others to look at, then placed it in a leather pouch which he wore around his waist.

Keithley told me later that that was the first time he had ever seen, much less heard of, any Indian putting something in his medicine pouch without it being done in secret. He said, "The power goes out of a medicine pouch if anyone else knows what is in it, but the old chief said that your medicine was too strong to be overcome, so it didn't matter that others had seen him put it in."

I asked, "Does that mean that I can look and see what is in the bag that he gave me?"

Keithley looked at me and said, "Well, 'Rockhand' Lizzie, that is entirely up to you. Curiosity belongs to the white man, and depending on how much of you is white, you will probably open it. But if you don't open it, it will mean that you're more Indian than you thought, and it will certainly be a mark of great respect to the old chief if you keep his sacred secret."

I tucked that medicine bag deep into my pocket and vowed never to open it, even if it meant I wouldn't be white anymore.

We got up early enough for me to have a good game of worshers before we left for Lamar and what we hoped was a reply from Kinsey. Remembering Keithley's "endgame" display at Hot Springs, I let their "hotshot" beat me in a close game, and then after we shook hands I took his worshers and mine, walked to the pitch line, and laid four air shots into the "five" hole. They were still staring at the worsher pit as we rode off.

Keithley asked with a big grin, "Did I teach you that?"

Keithley and I talked all the way to Holdenville, which was west of Horntown, about how we were going to make sure Robbins was caught dead to rights. I was nervous because Keithley had left the knife and baling wire in the box at Robbins's wagon. I was afraid they would disappear since Robbins knew somebody was on to him. I said something about it being a shame that we weren't trying to catch Cunningham, because we could use Jim for bait. Keithley looked at me, narrowed his eyes, then didn't say anything for several miles.

Then he whooped, and said, "I'll race you to the creek up ahead!" He got a head start on me, and besides, his horse was better than mine. When I plowed into the shade of the trees along the creek he was already off his horse, and insisted on helping me down. "That'll do it! That'll do it!" he cried.

"What'll do it?" I wanted to know.

Keithley explained to me that we needed to go by Wewoka, even if it was out of the way, because we needed to see Jim. Then he explained to me the idea he had. When I had said something about "bait," he said the idea hit him right between the eyes. I didn't like the idea, because it sounded too dangerous for Jim. After all, I was the one who had seen Miz Robbins with a fruit jar in her throat, and I had seen Mister Robbins when he was "crazy."

Keithley said, "Well, let's put it to Jim, wait for Kinsey, and see what he thinks. Then we'll decide."

We found Jim without any problem. He was really a fine-looking soldier, and had found a real home in the Seminole Nation. Even had him a girlfriend. We went to where he lived out on a hill just west of Wewoka. I poked around in the rocks while he and Keithley talked and planned. This whole hill was made out of funny rocks that looked like rattlesnake tails. I called Keithley over, and he said they were called fossils, and that they were all over the Indian Nation, in one shape or another. I guess that swung it for me. I decided I had to live out here, even if it meant traveling back and forth the rest of my life from crystals in Arkansas to fossils in the Indian Territory. Keithley looked at me and shook his head, as I went back to scrabbling around in the shale and gravel. I found one with a rock flower on the end of the stem, and saved it for Uncle Billy, if ever I got to see him again.

Jim talked to some of the other soldiers and to the Seminole chief for a long time that night. Next morning, he came riding over to where we were getting ready to go to Dustin, and said he was ready to go with us. He turned to me and said, "Don't you worry, Miz Lizzie. We're going to take care of this just fine."

Dustin had a hotel, but they wouldn't let Jim stay there, so we all went to the outskirts of town and stayed with some Indians who were camped there. The reply telegram from Kinsey said that he would arrive in Dustin today on the train. I stayed with Jim at the camp while Keithley went in to meet the train, and get Kinsey set up in the hotel.

They were a long time in coming back to the camp. I was waiting on a knoll, watching for them. I was mighty glad to see Kinsey, who looked just as sharp as ever in his Federal agent suit. When they came riding up, Kinsey said, "Well, Lizzie, you have turned into quite a traveler. And Keithley here tells me that's not all. I expected to see you wearing a feather head-dress, or maybe with war paint on."

After eating, Kinsey answered all my questions about Aunt Hettie, and what he knew about Uncle Billy, and said that before leaving Little Rock he had talked to Judge Boudreau, who was there for a convention. I mostly listened while the others laid their plans for the evening.

The protracted meeting was set up at the south end of town, under a large brush arbor, and near a campground down by the creek. Families had come in from the farms to stay for several nights, with someone trading off to go tend to chores. The preacher's wagon was at the edge of the camp, so he could "pray into the night" without disturbing others.

At nightfall the lanterns were burning, and people were drifting in to take seats and lay down pallets for the young. "Preacher" Robbins was back behind the arbor in a grove of trees with some other men praying for the "holy fire to fall" in the meeting. White folks sat in the middle, with Indians sitting over on the sides, and some blacks sprinkled through their midst. Most of the Indian men stood, with their blankets wrapped around them, but the younger ones hunkered or sprawled on the ground. The service was long enough that the lanterns had to be replenished with oil once. Finally there was some "exhorting" from back in the rear of the white section, and then it was "invitation" time. People responded by walking down to the front to kneel at a bench and then people would gather around to pray them through. When things got a little slack, a few shouts would get things started again.

Jim waited until a few blacks had already gone down, then he went down to the front. He was now dressed in some plain clothing, without his hat, and at first I didn't recognize him from where I sat at the back with an Indian family Keithley knew.

I could hear Robbins saying, "Oh, here is another child of darkness, coming into the light, cursed with the mark of Ham, but looking for the droppings from the white man's table." He stopped in front of where Jim was kneeling at the bench, and said, "Stand on yore feet, you child of sin! Confess to what is hidden in yore black heart. Maybe God will have mercy on you."

Jim stood up and said, "I done wrong! I done wrong! I ran away from those who needed me. I left a pore ole invalid woman back in Arkansas, who needed me to take care of her. Oh, my heart is heavy!"

I saw Robbins look at Jim, then turn him so that the light struck his face to advantage. "Nigger, where did you run away from? Who is that pore woman who was depending on you?"

The crowd of people were listening closely, and Jim said just loud enough to be heard in a choking voice, "Preacher, sar, it war in Arkansas, sar, Perry, Arkansas, sar."

Robbins thundered, "Didn't you hear me, nigger? I said, 'Who was that pore invalid you deserted?'"

Jim answered, "Oh, sar, her name is Miz Polly, sar."

I looked around for Kinsey, but couldn't locate him, so I just laid low, and prayed. Robbins was saying, "This son of perdition is in much need of prayer. Let's all turn in and get some rest, except for me. I, a man of God, am going to take this benighted sinner with the smell of Hell upon him, and retreat yonder and pray for his soul."

I watched as Robbins took Jim by the arm and escorted him out of the circle of light and towards his wagon. Some of the faithful doused the lanterns, and the crowd filed away to their rest. The Indian family I was with was leaving, and I was alone. I found a rock and turned it over in my hand, but having no target, I relaxed my grip. I didn't drop it though, as I moved slowly towards Robbins's tent, fearful of what we had got Jim into.

It sure was a funny prayer I heard Robbins offering over Jim. "You theiving, no-count nigger, I ought to cut your throat right here," he snarled, "and I may just do that, if I hear one peep out of you! Just wait till Cunningham gets his hands on you. It'll be my pleasure to see what he does to you. Hear that, nigger?"

I had crept up to where I could see Robbins's silhouette against the campfires in the distance. He was standing over a crumpled form, tying a gag on Jim. Then he jerked Jim to his feet, saying, "Get up, you black devil, we're going for a ride, a long ride. You ain't going to get away, neither. I've got just the thing to make you nice and comfortable. Ever hear of baling wire, nigger?"

It was all I could do to keep my hand still, and the rock cut into my hand as I clenched it hard. I strained to see, but mostly listened in the dark, while Robbins twanged the baling wire on the wagon boards as he tied up poor Jim with it. He hitched up his team, and quietly led them out of earshot of the camp. Then he climbed up on the wagon seat, singing, "I'm Just A Poor Wayfaring Stranger," and slowly began his way back in the direction of Arkansas and Perry.

It warn't hard to follow the noise of the wagon on the rough road, so I stayed a safe distance back, thankful again that Robbins didn't have a dog. After we had got well out of town, Robbins pulled off the road into an abandoned lane, unhitched the team, and rolled into his sack. My heart ached for Jim, and I thought more than once about trying to approach the wagon and loosen the gag and baling wire.

Then I sensed someone behind me, and I jumped and almost cried out. It was Keithley, walking and leading his horse. "Come on, Lizzie, Kinsey and I are camped just over the hill here. Let's get some sleep, we'll be back here before grey light. Then we'll see what the new day will bring."

Can you sleep when a friend is in trouble? Well, I felt guilty when I woke up, but I had been dog-tired. Keithley and Kinsey were saddling up the horses in the predawn, and discussing strategy. We rode for a while, then they gave me the reins and told me to wait with the horses, until I heard them whistle me up.

"How long will it be?" I asked.

"Not long," said Kinsey. "I've a feeling that come sun-up Robbins is going to want to look over his catch, and have a little enjoyment before he hitches up to ride."

I decided I warn't going to miss that. I led the horses to water, then hobbled them in some rich grass near the creek. I ran a rope through their pommel rings and tied that to a branch of the only tree in the glade, just for extra insurance. Then I took off in the direction of Robbins's wagon.

I got to the edge of the clearing where Robbins had stopped, just as he threw the flap back from the tailgate, and dragged Jim out onto the ground. He took off the gag, and said, "Now, nigger, you can holler if you want to, but every time you do, I'm going to make you wish you hadn't. Just to help you repent from all yore sinful wrongdoings, though they be many, I'm gonna chase those devils out of you with my whip! You hear me? By the time I get you back to Cunningham, you are gonna be one good nigger."

Robbins had reached inside the back of the wagon and was hunting his whip when Jim said, "You got me all baling-wired up, are you gonna knife me too?"

Robbins whirled around and hissed, "What did you say? Who told you ... what did you say?"

Jim said, "I was just wondering if you was brave enough to kill a man, to cut his throat, with him looking you in the eye?"

Robbins scrabbled around in the back of the wagon, found the box, jerked out the butcher knife, and leaped toward Jim, then stopped. "Ah, so you don't want to go home, huh? Thought you would cheat me out of what I'll get if I turn you over to Cunningham. You can't trick me, you cunning nigger. But take a look," he said, brandishing the knife, "Do you think I'm afraid of slicing me some dark meat? I've done it before, and I can do it again. Yore blood will look just as red as those three whites I killed out from Hollis." He skewered the knife into the sideboard of the wagon, turned back to pick up his whip, and stopped.

Standing at the tailgate of the wagon was Keithley, flanked by several Lighthorsemen from the Seminole Nation, in full uniform.

"Who are you? Where did you come from?" quavered Robbins. Keithley didn't say a word, but stepped forward and carefully removed the knife from the wagon sideboard, turned it over, looking at it in the increasing morning light, then placed it back in the box in the rear of the wagon. Robbins said, "You didn't answer me. Who are you, and who are these heathen Indians dressed up in uniforms? I'm just a God-fearing servant, returning this fugitive from justice to the authorities back in Arkansas."

Two of the policemen had flanked Robbins, backing him against a tree. He let the whip fall to the ground. Another stripped Robbins down to the waist. Keithley stepped in front of Robbins and said, "I'm a half-breed heathen, and I would like to tear yore heart out and eat it, if I didn't think it would make me sick. These are the Lighthorsemen of the Seminole Nation, who are looking for one of their missing policemen. They don't speak English, but they do seem to understand that you have tied up and kidnapped one of their men. You are also in the jurisdiction of the Seminole Nation. I don't know what they are going to do to you, but I think I'll stay and listen to you pray. You do know how to do that, don't you?"

Several of the other Lighthorsemen had gently unwired Jim, put some axle grease on his ankles and wrists, and helped him into his uniform. Then they twisted the baling wire around one of Robbins' wrists, then looped the loose end around the tree and bound his other wrist. One soldier picked up the whip Robbins had dropped, looked at it critically, compared it with his own, then turned and handed Robbins's whip to Jim. "You whip," he said.

At that Keithley stepped forward and said something to the Lighthorsemen in their language. They did not look pleased, but seemed to understand. One stepped over to Jim, took the whip, and moved towards Robbins. He brought the whip crashing down on Robbins's back, again and again. After each stroke, Keithley, who was standing near to Robbins, and looking into his distended eyes, said, "Say Amen!"

After about a half dozen strokes, Robbins began to repeat, "Amen!" at Keithley's direction. The next soldier took the whip, and the agony was repeated. Each time Keithley's refrain was, "Say Amen!"

After all the soldiers but Jim had laid open Robbins' back, Keithley stepped forward to say, "Did I hear you say this fine morning that you cut some white men's throats in Arkansas? If that be true, the only way you are going to stop this whipping is to sign a paper saying what you did and how and when and where."

Mister Robbins was right agreeable. They had just got that paperwork done, when Kinsey came up from the other side of the wagon. "What is going on here?" he asked, although he already knew the whole story. "Who is this man, and what has he done?"

Robbins was in no shape to talk, so Keithley introduced himself to Kinsey, explained that the "prisoner" had kidnapped one of the Seminole Nation Lighthorsemen, and was torturing him on Reservation land. "Properly speaking, this pore beggar is entitled to be brought before the

Council for trial, which I am safe in saying will result in execution," Keithley said. "This whipping he's getting is the lesser of two evils. And you will notice that the kidnapped soldier has not had a part in his punishment."

Kinsey took the offered confession, read it, asked Robbins if that was his signature, and was the statement true. Robbins started blubbering, "They railroaded me! I just signed that to keep them from murdering me!"

Kinsey replied, "Well, in that case, you are within your rights to insist on a trial, but it will have to be before the Seminole Nation Council, since you're on their land, and they have caught you red-handed. I have no jurisdiction or help to offer. I thought if this written statement was true, then I had a prior claim on you, because the reason I'm out here is to serve a warrant for your arrest and take you back to Arkansas for questioning. I guess I'll just have to wait my turn, until the Indian court gets through with you."

One of the policemen was snapping the whip, practicing snipping off twigs from some weeds. Robbins jumped at each crack of the whip, then winced at the bite of the baling wire. His eyes were wild, staring first at Keithley over his shoulder, then at Kinsey. He was measuring his chances.

"Let me loose, just untie me and get me out of here," he pleaded. "I don't want to go to Indian court and have a bunch of savages cutting me to ribbons."

Kinsey said in a reasoning tone, "Well, that's not really the issue here. The question is, 'Is this confession you signed a while ago true, or is it not?' I can't take you to Arkansas, and I don't think these folks are going to let me take you, unless you swear that your signed confession is the truth."

Robbins snarled at them all, "Yes, I killed them, they didn't mean anything to me, I was just doing what I was told to do. I'll go back and face the music in Arkansas. You can't convict me there anyway. I'm a man of God, and I've got friends in high places."

Kinsey said, "Well, I guess I'm satisfied with that, if these folks are.

What do you think, Keithley, can you explain it to these policemen so they can understand?"

Keithley palavered with the policemen, and came back after a while, saying, "They insist on conducting this gent to the train with you. It's not that they don't trust you or your credentials, they just want the town people to see them functioning. I think it's a pretty good idea, myself. I think that's from one of his sermons that he preached about some Old Testament character named Haman in the white man's Book. Near as I can remember that heathen prepared a gallows for his enemy and got hanged on it hisself. Since this policeman was taken out of town trussed up with baling wire, they are going to take the preacher back trussed up in baling wire. They won't give an inch on that."

I had heard plenty, but I was rehearsing what I had heard Robbins say about those three men at Hollis. He said something about "doing what he was told." What did that mean? They were loading Robbins into the wagon, trussed like a hog, gag and all, and I was hanging around the tailgate watching. Robbins tried to give a last kick in protest, and in the process knocked a cardboard box out onto the ground. I picked it up, saw that the butcher knife and coiled baling wire had fallen out. Kinsey asked me to pick them up and try to tie the lid on tight, and he would put them in his saddlebag.

I picked up the box, which was slightly the worse for wear, turned it over, then looked inside to see if there was anything else in the tissue paper. Nothing there, but I turned the box around and looked at the end. It was stamped with a shoe manufacturer's name and address, and printed in the bottom corner of the label was a name: *Cunningham's Store, Perry, Arkansas.* I did a brown study on that one, then took and showed it to Kinsey. He looked at it silently, then gave me a quizzical look.

"Lizzie, I think you have just tied another piece of baling wire around this case. I could wish that you could find a note from Cunningham to Robbins saying, 'Kill those three agents, and frame Billy Bean,' but that is too much to hope for. This runs a close second, though. I think the big happy family of Cunningham, Haskins, and Robbins is headed for a rocky reunion."

We rode into Dustin like a parade. At a brief stop on the outskirts, I had taken some charcoal from a dead fire we passed, and had written on the sides of the wagon sheets, "The Baling Wire Man." A goodly number of his converts came down to see us off. Robbins was minus the wire, but Kinsey had him wearing some steel handcuffs. Nobody had mentioned the wagon and team, but I saw Keithley making a deal with the stable down the street, then come back and hand me a pouch through the window, saying, "Lizzie, when you get ready to come back, send me a wire in care of the dispatcher at Lamar, and I'll meet you. I'll go by yore folks' place and let them know where you're off to, and why. Just don't get rusty with those worshers, hear?"

GERALD EUGENE NATHAN STONE

CHAPTER EIGHTEEN

JUDGE BOUDREAU WAS AT THE STATION IN HOT SPRINGS WHEN WE ARRIVED
early the next morning. Kinsey left Robbins cuffed around a pole at
the edge of the platform while he entered into a long, low conversation
with the Judge. I said to Robbins as I went down the steps, "You want me
to tell Mister Cunningham and Haskins that the 'Fruit Jar Man' has
arrived, or the 'Baling Wire Man'?"

Robbins snarled, and tried to jerk the pole out of its housing. "You
Samaritan puppy, just wait till I get loose the next time! You'll remember
them words!" I sniffed at him, but somewhere inside, cold water ran over
my heart.

Then I saw Aunt Hettie! We ran toward each other, and did a dance
on the train platform, around and around. Kinsey and the Judge stopped
and were watching us. "Now that's a pleasure to see," said the Judge.
"Lizzie, is that an Indian war dance, or have you come back peaceful-like
this time?" I sniffed and grabbed Aunt Hettie's arm to walk off under the
trees and tell her about my family.

After Kinsey and the Judge finished their conversation, and Robbins
had been carted off to jail, we all went to the Judge's house and Miz
Sammy fixed us a fine meal. After supper, the Judge said, "Well, Lizzie,

I'm sure you know that you're still legally a charge of Mister Cunningham's, and that coming back here creates a predicament for me. I know why you came, and I think that with a little luck, we can work things out. However, it will be touch and go, and I think you need to lay low for a while—no rock-throwing, no screaming, no worsher games. I hope we can get Cunningham's mind off of you, while we turn the fox loose in his henhouse. If the Court finds him and Haskins mixed up in that triple murder, then you will be free to go live with your brother in the Indian Territory. The trick is going to be making sure that those three bedfellows, Haskins, Cunningham, and Robbins, wear their fingers out pointing at each other. I've issued a warrant for their arrest, and they are going to be kept in separate jails, so they can't cook up a story together. Since there's no one in the women's ward, we put Robbins there, and when we get the other two they will be on separate floors in the main jail. There is a lawyer here in town that knows the story and wants to take Uncle Billy's case, which is being reopened."

Later I asked Kinsey, "What can go wrong? Why wouldn't they let Uncle Billy out, and put those three where they belong?"

Kinsey turned to me and said, "Lizzie, learn it now: Pure justice is hard to come by. Even those on the right side of the law sometimes twist or hide the facts in order to justify their actions. When this trial starts back up, you are going to hear a lot about that pore old invalid wife, the long-suffering sister, the atheistic moonshiner, the incorrigible juvenile, the misunderstood man of God, and the upstanding gentlemen of Perry. This lawyer that wants to take Uncle Billy's case is not going to fight fair either. He will use every trick he can think of, just like the other side."

Well, I guess that is how it would have been, but Robbins escaped that night. He apparently asked the trusty for a Bible, and was showing him the plan of salvation, like, "Here, come closer and read it for yoreself," and then grabbed the trusty's neck and hung on until he was senseless, got his keys, and flew the coop. They found the women's cell empty, and the trusty almost dead early next morning. No doubt he was thinking the less of religion.

Kinsey came for us at the Judge's house, where Aunt Hettie and I had spent the night, saying, "I can't believe it! We catch him, and get him all the way to Hot Springs, and they can't even keep him in the cell long enough to get the bench warm! Well, there's no help for it now. Hettie, I'm putting you on the train for Horntown, where Keithley will meet you and take you out to stay with Lizzie's folks. Lizzie I am keeping as close to me as a sticktight. I've spent the last hour trying to imagine what Robbins is going to do, and where he is going to go. I want to check some ideas with you, Lizzie, as soon as we get Hettie on that train and out of danger."

Cold water was still running over my heart as I watched Aunt Hettie disappear in the distance. I was relieved to see her get out of town, but it made me mighty lonely.

Kinsey didn't have any problem keeping me close to him. We ate a late breakfast on Bathhouse Row, sitting out in a little side yard with an umbrella over the table. Kinsey moved his plate after eating, put his elbows on the table, and said, "Now, Lizzie, let's figure out what Robbins may have up his sleeve. He's mad at Keithley and Jim, but they are too far away right now. He's mad at me for bringing him back to Arkansas, and that counts for something, and I'm going to keep my eye on my back trail. He's mad at Haskins and Cunningham for getting him into this situation to start with. And he's mad at you for a multitude of good reasons, last of which is that taunt you gave him when you got off the train. I don't mean to scare you, but I think he will come after you. And I'm afraid that it won't be to deliver you to Cunningham. What do you think?"

I said, "Kinsey, quit looking at me, and keep your eyes peeled behind me. That's what I'm doing for you. I'm scared, but mad, too. I feel like he's somewhere around here, watching us right now. Can we go somewhere else?"

After we paid our bill, we went to a small tourist overlook on a mountain looking down over the town. The place was alive with couples and tourists, sitting on benches and looking through telescopes, so I felt a little safer.

Kinsey said, "All right, Lizzie, what do you think Robbins will do?"

I had been thinking about that and was ready with my answer, "When Robbins got out of that jail, he took the trusty's gun, I expect. But I don't think he will be comfortable until he gets him a good sharp knife, and some more baling wire. I'm thinking that he will head back to his home place, then Perry, to pick a bone or two with Haskins and Cunningham. He can get all the baling wire he wants there, plus another knife. Then I think he'll pick his sweet time setting a trap for you and me. I know the Judge said for me to lay low, but we need to follow him now, before he has any idea we are in his neck of the woods."

So it was that we horsed up and lit out for Dripping Springs. We asked around a little, and a family there for the "cure" said, "Yes, a tall angry man came through earlier this morning, quoting Scripture." We headed for Hollis, going in by the old log road that I knew about. It took longer, but we knew we couldn't beat Robbins there anyway, and it would save us from stumbling into an ambush. We stood at the dike of outcropping just south and east of Hollis and looked down on the clearing in front of the store. There was Robbins in front of the store, taking his leave of someone who looked like Oren Blasingame, but I warn't sure. After Robbins mounted up and rode away, we went down the mountain and came in at the back door of the store.

It *had* been Oren. Oren had been looking after Uncle Billy's place while he was gone, and feeding the dogs. He had one of them with him on the porch, our old brindle bitch Xerxes. She jumped straight up from a sound sleep and lit out toward me like a dog half her age, and nearly knocked me over licking and whimpering. He had been sitting by the window, looking out, and whittling on a pine knot. He jumped when he saw Xerxes bolt, then relaxed when he saw us, saying, "Miz Lizzie, I'm glad to see you, but I'm mighty glad you warn't here about half an hour ago. There's trouble hunting the hills—Satan hisself was just here."

I said, "Yes, we know, Oren, we were watching from the dike. What did you find out?"

Oren responded, "Well, I knew he wouldn't tell me directly where he was off to, so when he got ready to go, I handed him a couple of letters and asked him to give them to Haskins. He reached out and took them without thinking, then caught himself and said, 'I don't reckon I'll be seeing him—I'm going up north toward Nimrod.' He slapped the letters down on the counter, and was messing around looking in the knife case, then he left. After he left I came back in to put the letters up, and they were gone. I knew then that he was headed straight to Perry, and more particularly, he was on his way to see Haskins and Cunningham."

As Kinsey and I rode away, we took Xerxes with us. We had no choice—she wouldn't go back to Oren when he called. Kinsey said, "That Oren is a conniver just like you, Lizzie."

I smiled at him and said, "It takes one to know one, Kinsey."

Again, we took the longer road, one I felt like Robbins would not take, but which led eventually to the cemetery on the sharp little hill overlooking Perry—the same one I had hid out on before taking off for Indian Territory. I turned to Kinsey, and asked, "Do you have a plan? What are we going to do next?"

Kinsey looked at me and said, "I thought *you* had the plan, Lizzie."

I guess that is what I liked so much about Kinsey. He was so quick to turn a serious situation into something funny. I made a face at him, but kept my eyes peeled on the Cunningham store below. Robbins's horse was hitched at the rear, so I figured he would be coming out the back door anytime now.

He came out all right, but he had Miz Sally with him, holding her wrist and making her walk alongside of him. It looked like from where we were that Miz Sally was in pain, so I sighed and said to Kinsey, "Well, I guess he found some baling wire all right, he's got some looped around Miz Sally's wrist."

We watched as they went down the road to the Cunningham house, then went in. "I wonder where Mister Cunningham is, Kinsey?" I thought out loud. "It's not like a murderer to just walk down the street in broad daylight, even if he is crazy as a loon."

Kinsey said, "Well, we can't easily handle all three of them, though I had just as soon have all three in front of me as to have only two and wonder where the third one was. Do you think we can get down there without being seen? And do you think you can handle that brindle and keep her quiet?"

It made for a lot of walking, but we stayed behind the dense cedars growing in the fencelines It sure made me glad that birds like cedar berries, and that they had planted these seed years before. We snuck around to the east side of the Cunningham place, and came up behind Jim's old shack. The back door was open just wide enough for us to squeeze through without having to run the danger of a squealing hinge. Xerxes was quiet, but the chickens in the back yard clucked a little bit, not sure whether there was danger in the back yard or not. We lay low until the chickens settled down, then moved to peep through the cracks in the siding. I could see the yard warn't well kept, and some clothes on the line looked like they had been there for weeks. All of Miz Polly's windows were in plain sight, and I could see her on her bed, but not looking our direction.

It was beginning to rain, so that meant the chickens would go to roost, and wouldn't be a problem if we wanted to go near the house. I had no idea what we were going to do next, but didn't have time to ask Kinsey what his idea was, because Miz Polly started her fly swatter. She was rattling it on the iron bedstead, louder than the rain on the tin roof. Then we could see two people come to the bedroom door, and one was a woman, so it had to be Robbins, still holding on to Miz Sally with his baling wire handcuffs. We heard a buggy cross the railroad tracks and turn into the yard. It was Mister Cunningham and he had Haskins with him. Haskins jumped out and got on the porch to get out of the rain, and Mister Cunningham let the horse have its lead to head for the barn. Fine! Right next to where we were. We hunkered low, and I kept my hand around Xerxes' muzzle.

I thought to myself that I was sure doing a lot more praying lately. My teeth were chattering a little bit, too. Kinsey placed a hand on my pigtails and gave a reassuring tug, and my heebie-jeebies passed. Mister Cunningham didn't do much for his horse, no rubdown or nothing, just took him out of his harness and slapped him into the stall. Then he ran for the back porch where Haskins was waiting. The two of them went in the back door, then stopped dead in their tracks without closing the door—they had seen Robbins and Miz Sally standing half in the hall and half in Miz Polly's room.

Kinsey motioned to me, saying, "Now, while their attention is on each other, let's move up to the other end of the porch." That was sorta like saying, "Let's stand a little closer to this rattlesnake," but I obeyed. We made it to the porch, and stood with our backs to the wall beside the door, listening to the happy family inside.

Miz Polly was rattling her fly swatter, demanding attention. Miz Sally was furious, and saying, "Let me loose, you crazy fool!" Robbins was saying, "Shut up! I'll slit yore throat if you don't!" Cunningham was saying, "Now, Robbins! Now, Robbins! What in tarnation are you doing?"

Haskins was slowly backing out the door, when Robbins cracked at him, "Hold it right there, Haskins, or I'll drill you right in the gut! Git right back in here, both of you, come on in here with this ole biddy in the bed. Move!"

"Now then, brethren, just have a seat," said Robbins in his preaching voice. "We'll just let these dear sisters sing for us, and then we'll see who wants to come to the mourners' bench. You, Haskins! Take this here baling wire and tie Cunningham to his dear wife's side—right there to that iron bedstead. That's it! Tighter! Twist it agin! Now, dear sister, you are going to tie Brother Haskins's hands to the other bedpost. Hurry up about it. Now! Don't that look like one happy family? Come back over here, Sister Sally, you need to be near yore dear sister's head, that's right, right by the other bedpost. It's a pity I don't have that nigger and that pigtailed brat here to tie to the other bedpost. But all in good time!"

We heard a chair being dragged from the kitchen, and heard it creak as Robbins seated himself in it. "Now, brethren and sisteren, let me ask you once, and only once: Who let that nigger get out of here, and who let that Tackett brat get out of here, and who let them track me down in the Indian Territory, and who let them drag me back to Hot Springs? Did you know they know who had me kill those three agents up near Billy Bean's cabin? Do you have any idea how unhappy that makes me?"

We heard a gasp from Miz Sally, "Oh, you cold-blooded murderer! And not just you! All of you! You planned this! You swine!"

The chair scooted back as Robbins jumped to his feet, "You swiveled bitch! You'll pay for that!"

I bent down and hissed in Xerxes' ear, *"Siccum!"*

A brindle blur hit Robbins from the rear. Robbins roared, trying to turn around and club his revolver at the dog. He fell back against Miz Polly's bed, kicking at Xerxes, trying to get a bead on the dog, but was afraid of shooting himself. I dashed into the room intent on protecting my dog, with Kinsey right behind me. A mighty swat from Robbins stunned Xerxes, and she rolled into the middle of the room.

Then that son of a biscuit eater shot my dog right before my eyes, and raised his gun to me.

Several things happened at once, or at least close together. Miz Polly dropped her fly swatter, grabbed a knife out of Robbins's belt, and slashed him just below the shoulder blade; Robbins's gun went off; and I fell on my dying dog in tears. What was meant for me hit Kinsey instead, right through the shoulder. Robbins, staggering and bleeding, stumbled out the door, and off into the gloom of evening.

Miz Sally was screaming, and the tied-up men were tugging at the wire, saying, "Untie me! Untie me!" I raised my head from Xerxes, looked at them, then turned at a groan from Kinsey as he rose from the floor and staggered out the door in pursuit of Robbins. Miz Polly had dropped the knife with a clatter on the floor, and was rattling her fly swatter once more, wailing, "I want my nigger! Whar's my nigger?"

I left them where they were, and turned to follow Kinsey. I had no dog to help me now. For sure I couldn't holler and let Robbins know my whereabouts. But I had to find Kinsey and help him, because he was bad hurt, and Robbins would probably try to ambush him.

I headed for the barn, figuring that Robbins would grab the buggy and light out of these parts, and Kinsey must have figured the same. Halfway there I heard a terrific struggle going on by the horse stall. It had to be Robbins and Kinsey, two wounded men fighting for their lives. I heard the wind go out of someone, and Robbins's harsh cry, "Take that, and if it don't fit, here's another one." The sound of a boot cracking someone's head is a terrible sound.

Robbins ranted on, "Tie me up, will you? I'll see if you know what that means, lawman. Here, taste some of this baling wire!" I could hear him trussing Kinsey up, and then I saw him drag Kinsey's limp body out of the shadows to the buggy. Panting, he bent over to get his breath, finished hitching the horse, then he hesitated, looking at the house, apparently giving thought to me and the rest. When he staggered, I figured he had decided to seat up and get out of the country.

I knew the yard—after all, I had left sweat in just about every corner of the premises. It was dark, but I ran around the opposite side of the house, knowing what I had to find. I felt around under the edge of the front porch for what I wanted, and as Robbins swept by with reins let out over the horse's back, I let fly with a stout bean pole. It went through the buggy wheel nearest me, and as the spokes carried it up to the buggy bed, there was a loud clap, the buggy skewed around to the left, and Robbins flew over the transom.

In the dim glow from the lights in the house I saw Robbins hit the ground, roll over and lay there, and I said, "That's for Uncle Billy!"

To my horror, Robbins raised his head, shook it, got up slowly and moved towards me. "You think I can't see you, don't you, you little spawn of the devil. I'm going to get you now, and you're going to die slow."

I should have known it would come down to this. I found this rock in my hand, but needed to get him off balance, so I wheeled and took off running. When I heard him in full pursuit, I stopped dead in my tracks, turned and let fly. He conveniently tried to turn his head to avoid whatever I was throwing, and the rock caught him right in the temple. He went down like a sack of manure in the pouring rain.

I didn't bother untying Kinsey first. I ran to the buggy, and found some loose baling wire on the floor board, and hurried back to Robbins.

I tied him up myself, good and tight, and left him face down in the rain. Then I went and untied Kinsey, and we sat there on the tailgate of the buggy, leaning against one another in the rain. I think we both cried a little bit—I know I did. Then Kinsey unhitched the horse, slapped him on the flank, and let him seek his own pasture. We turned and went towards the house. Kinsey was leaning on me a little harder than he probably thought he was, but I didn't mind. He'd sure been there for me when I needed to lean on him.

We loosed Miz Sally first, and she sank to the floor, staring at nothing in particular for several minutes, then she got up and said, "Oh, Polly, you were so brave!" She turned to look at Mister Cunningham and Haskins, still snug against the bed posts, and spat, "I hope you both rot in prison!" Then she turned to me with a sad smile, saying, "Miz Lizzie, I need to change my sister's sheets. Would you mind bringing me some clean sheets, please?" Since she asked nice, I was happy to oblige.

It was almost train time, so Kinsey hobbled on down to the station to arrange passage for five, and send a couple of telegrams. As he left, he said, "I checked on Robbins but he's still out cold. Even if he wakes up, Lizzie's got him so well wired, he'll not be able to scratch his nose."

Miz Sally helped me wrap Xerxes in one of her storebought shawls, and I carried her out to where Robbins was, and noticed that he was watching me with the one eye that was above the water rising in the ruts. Water was running across the yard, under and around his body, mingling with rivulets of blood. I got a shovel from the barn and started digging in the pouring-down rain, right in front of him. I admit I tossed a little of the mud and dirt on Robbins, but it felt good. I could see him cringe and shake, staring wild-eyed at my digging, so I stopped and watched him for a breather.

"What...what are you doing?" he asked, and I answered him, "Digging a grave, what does it look like I'm doing?" After I got it deep enough, I turned to him again, saying, "Don't worry, this ain't yore grave. You don't deserve one, Mister Dog Killer!"

After I laid Xerxes to rest, and had patted the mud down smooth, I went over to Robbins, now lying in a goodly puddle of water as the rain kept on pouring down. I leaned on my shovel and asked sweetly, just as if we were at tea in the brush arbor, "Mister Baling Wire Man, tell me, do you favor sprinkling or immersion?"

CHAPTER NINETEEN

WE WARN'T A CIRCUS, BUT WE SURE FELT LIKE ONE. EVERYONE ON THE train stared at us, and the ones that couldn't see found plenty of excuses to get up and meander past our sideshow. Kinsey was in obvious pain, but he had our three exhibits securely handcuffed and shackled to the seat supports. Robbins had been taken out of his baling wire jewelry, but his wrists were raw and bleeding, and his head had a beautiful knot on it. Mister Cunningham and Haskins tried to sink down out of sight, which made them the more noticeable. They tried to keep their hats pulled down over their eyes, but when they slid off, I sure didn't bother to pick them up. Of the five of us, Kinsey, Robbins and I were still dripping wet. I wrung my braids, and pulled the blanket around me that Miz Sally had insisted on me taking. What came over that woman was really something to see, which I guess proves that something good can come out of even Perry.

We stopped in Ola to make the switching change for Hot Springs, and a peddler got on who looked familiar to me. As he came down the aisle we recognized each other at the same time. It was my previous acquaintance who "taught" me to play checkers. He stopped, pushed his hat back, and said, "Now let me guess, don't tell me ... you're off to the

Indian Territory again, and looking for some pore jasper to sucker into a game."

I sniffed and replied, "Well. not quite, but that's close. If you don't mind where you sit, and really want to play a game, you can sit next to Mister Baling Wire there."

Kinsey had opened one eye, and was watching and listening. My checker friend said, "Waal, you look like you're full of a story, so I'll just sit by this gent, as long as he don't have hydrophobia. Tell me what's going on with you, young lady." He gestured to the handcuffed three and asked, "And is this a collection of your winnings?"

After he introduced himself to Kinsey, and explained how he knew me, he began to pump me about what I had been doing. Kinsey shook his head, and settled back to try and sleep. It took a long time to tell, because of the grunts and squirms from the prisoners, but I had a big-eared listener. When I got to the part about Xerxes, "Mister Checkers" slapped his hat on the floor, stood up, swore, and turned around to face Robbins. I guess all the vinegar had leached out of Robbins lying there in the rain in Cunningham's yard, because he just shrank up in the corner of the seat. "You should have buried him with the dog! Now that would have been a reversal of Indian custom, wouldn't it?"

I asked, "What do you mean?" and he explained that Indians sometimes killed a horse or dog to bury with a fallen brave—or so he had heard. I decided to ask Keithley next time I saw him.

"Well, who is going to run the store, with this here gent going out of town?"

I said, "I don't know or care, but I guess Miz Sally can handle everything pretty much on her own. I do know she don't want any help from these jaspers, except maybe that one there to sweep out, or empty the spittoons. But he ain't going to be doing that kind of work anytime soon, if what Kinsey says is true. He'll be crushing rock in the prison yard. I sure hope Uncle Billy saved him some good ones."

We were met at the station by Judge Boudreau and the local sheriff. As they got ready to march the trussed-up trio off to jail, I called out to the sheriff, "Be sure that jasper there don't ask for no Bible." The sheriff turned, looked at me and spat, "Don't you worry none on that score. I'm putting the same trusty on duty that had him the last time, and he has definitely turned agin religion."

The next week was a whirlwind. There were people from Little Rock who came to town with pencils behind their ears. Various groups representing temperance societies were there, the Grand Master of the Lodge was there, and even a tall, skinny scarecrow from the Little Rock Orphanage. I didn't like the way he looked at me, so I stuck close to either Aunt Hettie or Kinsey.

They had brought Uncle Billy back from the prison, and were ready to turn him loose on his own "recognizance," whatever that meant, but Uncle Billy would have none of it. He insisted on being housed in the jail, asking to be put in the cell with any one of the jaspers we had brought in, it didn't matter which one. But the sheriff warn't dumb—I guess he could see Uncle Billy's fingers curling. But he did consent to put him across the corridor in the drunk tank, where Uncle Bill could look them in the eye and share a few choice words with them. That's the way Kinsey described it to me.

Since they were being tried together, and nobody wanted any part of Robbins, they couldn't get a lawyer to represent them, so the Judge appointed one. I suppose it warn't no accident that he chose the same lawyer that had represented Uncle Billy in his trial. Of course, we didn't have a lawyer this time, since the prosecuting attorney was primed and ready to go after his new targets.

Kinsey said, "Lizzie, I think it would be a good idea for you to just sit still this time. Don't throw anything, no worshers, and no lawyer-baiting." I said that was fine by me, so when the prosecuting attorney glanced at me during his opening statement, I just smiled at him. He stopped, trying to remember what he had been saying, couldn't, and finished lamely.

They brought Uncle Billy in and gave him a seat off to the side, facing across the room to the jury, where he had a good view of the witness chair. He looked thin, and had a worrisome cough, but his eyes had the old sparkle. That is, except when he looked at the defendants' table, then a cloud came over his face, and his eyes turned to cold slate.

I had my first opportunity to get close to Uncle Billy during the noon recess. He held me at arm's length for a while, then buried his face in my hair as I wept into his beard. We walked out to the worsher pits, and stood there for a while looking at them. Some boy came up and offered us his worshers, and Uncle Billy said, "Shore, why not?" We pitched, then walked to the other end, arm in arm, where we pitched again. Back and forth. Didn't even keep score. Sometimes I couldn't see the holes for my tears. The few watchers got disgusted and left us to pitch alone.

"Uncle Billy, when can we go home?" I asked when I could finally talk.

Uncle Billy looked up at the mountains surrounding the town, coughed, and said, "Soon, Lizzie, soon. But first, after this trial is over, I got a little trip I'd like to make." When my face clouded up, he punched me and said, "With you, of course. I had a cell mate down at the prison who was telling me about a rockhound he knew down round Murfreesboro. I think you and I orta go down that way and mosey around a bit. You think another rock fling would be good for us?"

As we walked back to the courtroom, I asked, "What about Aunt Hettie, Uncle Billy? Will she want to come, too? She'll be down in the mouth with us gone, you know."

Uncle Billy didn't answer right away, then he said, "Lizzie, she's got a lot on her mind right now. I'll talk to you about that later. Right now it's time for court to start."

Well, my pot simmered about that the rest of the trial. What could Uncle Billy mean? Something was wrong, and I didn't know what it was.

They sentenced Robbins to hang, and gave Haskins and Cunningham ten years of hard labor. I looked over at Uncle Billy, remembering what he had said to those two at his own trial, about what he would do if they ever laid a hand on me. I was puzzled at seeing him smile, until Kinsey leaned over and told me that the inmates at the penitentiary knew the whole story from Uncle Billy, and were pretty anxious to have Haskins and Cunningham stay with them for awhile.

We stopped by the store in Hollis and talked to Oren, or at least we tried to. Uncle Billy's hounds just about went crazy when they saw Uncle Billy. They were spreading their joy all around, and I stayed out of their way, but Uncle Billy had to change his overalls before we left for the cabin. I told Aunt Hettie that Xerxes wouldn't have done that, but then she was a girl, and smarter. Aunt Hettie laughed with pure delight, which kind of made up for that empty feeling at not having Xerxes any more.

When we got to the cabin, I drew a fresh bucket of water, and we stood there looking out over the place. What more could a body want? Mountains, a cabin, hounds, and a well of cold, sweet water. It didn't take much prodding, but I made Uncle Billy and Aunt Hettie sit down on the porch in their rockers, and I flew around doing chores, getting a fire startted for supper, stopping to chunk a few rocks out of sheer exhuberance. No Robbins, no Haskins, and no Cunningham. Back together with Uncle Billy and Aunt Hettie, and rock hunting ahead!

Then I noticed that the rockers had stopped, and then I heard Aunt Hettie crying, and Uncle Billy saying, "Hesh now! Hesh now, Hettie. Crying ain't gonna fix nothing."

I was confused again. What was going on? But I pushed it away, and started making noise in the kitchen. Soon enough I had cornbread and sliced onions ready to go with the canned crowders I had opened and heated with a chunk of fatback. Oren had given me a jug of sweet milk in case I couldn't rustle up old Lucy before dark, and sure enough, that high-falutin' Jersey had heisted her tail and taken off for the back fence. I hollered after her, "See if I care! Oren's Guernsey gives more milk than you do, anyway!"

Uncle Billy said grace before we ate, which surprised me. I couldn't remember that he had done that since Aunt Maud died. Maybe prison was good for him.

Next morning I was up early and had breakfast done and on the back of the stove before anyone else was up. I was sweeping the chicken mess out of the front yard when I heard Uncle Billy *kerplunk* the dipper back in the bucket. He said, "Well, do you want to go rock hunting, or not? The day is wasting."

I said, "Today? Already? You just got home, and you're ready to go, just like that?"

Uncle Billy said, "Just like that. After breakfast, that is."

Wonder of wonders! Aunt Hettie said she wanted to go, too. So we lit out about mid-morning, packing in a few vittles for the trip. Uncle Billy said that we wouldn't need to carry everything, since we were going to stop at Judge Boudreau's for the night, and Miz Sammy most likely would fix our traveling vittles for the trip on down to Murfreesboro.

It seemed like we were going to wear out that road to Hot Springs, but I looked forward to seeing the Judge again, and maybe get to prowl around in his house and see what else it held. After a brief stop at Dripping Springs, we wound on down the valley and arrived at Judge Boudreau's in time to look around outside before supper. The Judge had a fishpond he seemed to be proud of, and I reckon his fish were supposed to be pretty, but I couldn't find anything except their color to recommend them. I did notice, however, that the pond was built out of one of each kind of rock there probably was in the whole world. When those fish died, and the pond was torn up, I thought those rocks would look mighty good in a collection. I tested one of them that had star-like crystals embedded in it to see if it might be loose in the mortar, and the Judge hollered at me, "Lizzie, if you're looking for a rock to throw, get some out of the creek back there." I looked up and could see that he and Uncle Billy were having a pretty serious conversation. Aunt Hettie was with them, but seemed subdued and quiet.

Next day after Miz Sammy had fussed over us, loading us down with Tucker lard buckets full of still-warm food, we took off. We passed through some wild and wonderful rough country on our way to Murfreesboro, which Uncle Billy explained was not the easy route, but he wanted us to see the Little Missouri. Beyond that the land eased up and we came into town from the north. Uncle Billy said we would be visiting this rockhound he had heard about, by the name of Ed Hutchins. He lived out southeast of town, but we would stay in town for the night, and go there the next day.

Next morning we were out at the Hutchins place early. While Uncle Billy visited and introduced Aunt Hettie to Mister and Miz Hutchins, I mosied around the yard, and got acquainted with the hounds enough that they let me pull a few ticks off them, then together we examined the rock specimen piles in the yard. After a while, we excused ourselves, and went down into the rear pasture land.

We camped Aunt Hettie under a large honey locust with our lunches, so she could guard it from one of the Hutchins' hounds that had follered me. The field was cut with several erosion gullies that were working their way down to the creek, so it warn't hard to figure out where to start. Uncle Billy started down one of the shallow ravines, looking in the dried-up pools and hollows. I stopped under a large chinquapin that was at the edge of the ravine, and picked around the exposed roots on the downstream side. I never had seen so many different kinds of rocks in one place before, most of which I didn't recognize. Instead of playing a "Hey, look, what is this one?" game with Uncle Billy, I just stowed them in the Tucker bucket I had with me, and kept on digging.

Then I heard Uncle Billy sing out, "Lizzie, come on down hyar. I want to show you something." He had run into the same thing I had—different kinds of rocks, and some crystals, which I recognized. He said, "Lizzie, I want you to look at this agate, and here's a piece of red jasper. But especially, I want to show you something I ain't sure of. See, look at this yellow beauty! If it's what I think it is ... but it can't be, of course, but it shore does look like one. I saw some of these in a rock show in Hot Springs years ago, and the label said they were rough diamonds from Africa. That's the only place diamonds come from, you know. You don't suppose...?"

I turned it over, spit on it, and rubbed it on my dress, then held it up to the light. It was kinda small, compared with the crystals we were used to finding, but it was different, and pretty. I grabbed my Tucker bucket, fumbled around in it, and got a fair-sized rock I had gathered from under the tree root, gave it the spit treatment, and handed it to Uncle Billy, saying, "Trumps!"

He threw his hat down, and fumed, "Plague take it! Where did you get that ... that diamond?"

I said, "That chinkeypin is setting on them like a mother hen on a nest of eggs. Come on and I'll show you."

Aunt Hettie had roused herself from her reverie, and hearing our yelping, she met us at the chinquapin with the lunch. She insisted that we eat first, before doing anymore of that infernal digging, saying, "It's well enough that 'Hell is moved from beneath to meet you at your coming,' without you trying to meet it halfway."

Uncle Billy snorted, and said, "Wait till we get this chicken put away, then I'm gonna show you something you won't believe."

I don't think I ever saw Uncle Billy so happy, or so excited—it made Aunt Hettie nervous and she kept looking at me, then at Uncle Billy. Uncle Billy said presently, "All right now, Hettie, close yore eyes and make a big wish." While she did, Uncle Billy got up, took his new-found yellow stone between his thumb and first finger, went behind her and lowered it between her and the sun, then said, "Open 'em up, Hettie, and tell me what you see."

Aunt Hettie squinted at it, and said, "So you've found a piece of broken glass, have you? It's pretty, but not as pretty as your crystals."

Uncle Billy cackled, "Glass? Glass? You think this is glass?" He yelled and gave a little dance, saying, "I'm gonna take you to the jewelry store in Hot Springs and let you call all those sparkler rings in their showcases 'glass.' This here is a diamond, Hettie, let me show you." He took his Barlow and a couple of crystals out of his bib, laid them down, and said, "Watch!" Neither Aunt Hettie or I knew what he was doing, but he took that yellow stone and drew it across the crystal he had. It left a crease in the crystal facet. Then he took the Barlow, opened it and tried to cut a mark in the yellow stone. He sawed away at it, but nothing happened. "Hettie, a diamond is the hardest stone known to man. This is a pure-dee diamond, found by yours truly in these here United States, and you, Miz Hettie Bean, are the recipient of the first one ever found in this hemisphere!"

Aunt Hettie, and I guess, me too, looked at Uncle Billy like he was talking Indian. Aunt Hettie's jaw dropped, and she said, "William, you can't possibly mean that. It's a beautiful rock, but a diamond? I thought diamonds had facets."

Uncle Billy exploded, "They do, you sweet ninny, but they have to be cut—this is a diamond in the rough, right out of the womb of a patient Mother Earth, waiting for us to come along and play midwife." Then remembering what I had said about the nest under the chinquapin, he stopped, and said, "Come on, Hettie, let me show you—Lizzie says she's located a nest of them. Come on!"

We were so excited digging in that tree's resting place that we even had the hound trying to do his share, thinking we were on the trail of something that he couldn't smell. Suddenly Uncle Billy straightened up and went into a coughing fit. I didn't pay him much mind, but Aunt Hettie did, I guess. I became aware that me and the hound were the only ones digging. I turned to see Aunt Hettie white as a sheet, and Uncle Billy with blood down his beard and bib.

I jumped up, saying "What's wrong, Uncle Billy? Aunt Hettie, what's wrong?"

That was when we all sat down under the chinquapin, and Aunt Hettie explained to me that Uncle Billy was sick; he had what was called "T.B." Aunt Hettie talked about what the disease did, and that there was no cure. Apparently he had caught it in prison, and after getting out, Kinsey had caught him coughing up blood at the trial in Hot Springs, and had braced him about it. Uncle Billy had finally agreed to tell Aunt Hettie, but he couldn't bring himself to tell me. It was then I remembered Aunt Hettie crying on the front porch, and several other incidents when they didn't seem to be happy.

We packed up our rocks, filled in the holes, and made the long trip home in silence. We didn't talk, but I had a silent conversation going on all the way. I don't know whether I was talking to God or to Death, or to

Anything or Anyone out there who would listen. As we neared home, I hung back, and walked with the dogs who had come to meet us. Dogs are good listeners, so I poured out my woe to them. "It ain't fair! It ain't fair!" I cried. I sank down on an old fallen log beside the path, letting the hounds wash away my tears.

Aunt Hettie came back to find me, and hearing my protest about fairness, she said, "Lizzie, life isn't fair. Life is hard, life is about trouble, and grit, and bad times. But in between all those 'unfair' things that come our way, there is more than enough joy, and bravery, and good times. Those are the things that hold everything together. Come on and let's go to the house. Uncle Billy needs his 'country girl' very much now."

CHAPTER TWENTY

THE DAYS WENT BY LIKE A BLUR. I REMEMBER OREN COMING BY REGULAR to sit and visit with Uncle Billy, first on the front porch in the rockers, then later in the bedroom. Oren went to Hot Springs once and sent a wire to Kinsey. Uncle Billy told me to go to Hollis on the day that Kinsey was to arrive. When I saw him coming into town, I ran down the road to meet him and he swung me up into the saddle with him. I buried my face in his shoulder and cried most of the way to the place. Just like the other time, Kinsey stopped and said, "Now, Lizzie, it don't seem proper for us to be going up to the house with you looking like a swarm of yellowjackets has gotten after you. Let's stop here at the creek, and you wash some of that puffiness out of your face. Uncle Billy probably feels bad enough without seeing you bawling."

Kinsey stayed late into the night, sitting by the bed and drinking coffee with Uncle Billy. They had so many cups I figured it must be laced with something out of a jug. I had just about drowsed off when I heard Kinsey burst out, "No! No, I can't do that! It wouldn't be right. Get that notion out of your head right now." He stormed out into the dogtrot, and I could hear him breathing hard on the front porch. Then I heard him mount up and ride away to spend the night at Oren's.

Uncle Billy took a turn for the worse that night, and Aunt Hettie and I were up till dawn. He rallied after the sun came up, and spent some time talking to Aunt Hettie, who was quietly crying, making no reply. Then he called me in and talked about remembered times, various worsher games, rock hunting and finding this or that rock, and possum hunting. After that he began to ramble. He rallied again to tell me what to do with the diamonds we had found, not to tell anyone where we had found them, and when I was grown and married, to come back and buy that farm from Ed Hutchins. He put his hand on my head, tousled my braids, and said, "Lizzie, I know you will want to stay here and take care of Hettie, but I want you to go live with yore own folks. You've been a true partner, a real rockhound, and I thank God you crawled under my porch."

The next morning I stood at the head of the grave, and Oren was leaning on a shovel at the other end. Aunt Hettie was on one side of the grave holding some flowers, and Kinsey was on the other, rotating his hat around and around like the brim was too hot to hold. I waited for Kinsey to say something, or maybe Aunt Hettie. They were looking at each other: Aunt Hettie's face was white, and Kinsey's was red. It slowly dawned on me that what I had overheard during the night when Kinsey was sitting up with Uncle Billy was not a plea for Kinsey to end his life, which had been my wild guess, but he had been talking to Kinsey about Aunt Hettie. What a fool I had been! Uncle Billy was taking care of his soon-to-be widow, and had asked Kinsey to marry her after he was gone. And here, standing over Uncle Billy's grave, I could see it plain as day: They were made for each other, but probably didn't even know it yet. If they did know, it would be awhile before either of them would be ready to admit it.

Well, it looked like nobody was going to say anything, so I looked down at the plain lid of the pine coffin, swallowed a big lump in my throat, and began, "Death, here we are agin. You took my Pa and my Ma, then you took Aunt Maud, and my dog, and now you've done took my Uncle Billy. It ain't getting any easier."

"Amen," whispered Oren. I looked up and beyond him, toward the west . . . toward the Indian Territory . . . toward my folks and home.

Round about the end of that week, Kinsey and Aunt Hettie took me to Perry to catch the train for the Indian Territory. It seemed like a fitting place to leave from, although I felt a little different about it now that Xerxes was buried there in the Cunningham's yard. Somebody had planted some flowers on her grave, so I guess it must have been Miz Sally, which softened my thoughts for her even more. But I still didn't want to go to the house and listen to that fly swatter of Miz Polly's ever again.

Nor did I want to go to Cunningham's store, but I needed to get some things to take to my folks. So I went to the Commissary store down the street. There was a familiar-looking young man minding the store, though he warn't working that I could see. He had a book out on the cracker barrel and was reading it while he leaned on his broom.

I said to him, "Do you work here? If you ain't going to sweep the floor, why don't you do something useful like scrape the front yard, or build some worsher pits?"

He took a good look at me, cocked his head to the right, and smiled as he said, "I'll swan if it ain't Lizzie Tackett! Don't you remember me, Lizzie? I'm Mark, that went to school with you in Hollis. I'll never forget how you blistered Ted Gann's hand that day, throwing the baseball harder than any of us boys."

Well, to tell the truth, I didn't remember him, but I did remember Dickie Fulmer trying to get me to join the team that day. I decided not to tell Mark that, since it might have hurt his feelings and I didn't want to do that, even though I warn't ever going to see him again after today.

"You look dressed up for traveling," he said. "Where you headed?"

I replied, a little smugly, "I'm going to the Indian Territory."

"When are you coming back?"

"I ain't never coming back to Perry. Why do you want to know?"

He cocked his head to the left and said, "Oh, I just thought I'd ask. Well, then, if you ain't coming back here, I guess I'll just have to go out there."

The train whistled, and I had to leave. I took my purchases and ran to the station, where Aunt Hettie and Kinsey were standing on the platform. After hugs and kisses and a promise to come see me, they got me seated on the train—this time, with a ticket bought at the station.

Kinsey said with a wink as they left, "Good worsher-pitching to you, Lizzie, but don't bankrupt the whole Indian Territory before they have a chance to petition for statehood."

As the train pulled away from the station, I had a lot of things to think about: the sad memories of days past, the anticipation of the reunion with my folks, the excitement about a new place to live, and the hope of claiming a nest of real diamonds someday. And now I had one new thing to study. My thoughts kept wandering back to my visit to the Commissary Store, where a young man with more interest in a book than a broom had spoken words of promise: ". . . I guess I'll just have to go out there."

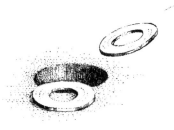

I STOOD BY MY WORD TO MARK AT THE COMMISSARY STORE THAT DAY: I
haven't been back to Perry, and I don't ever intend to go. Jake went back
for a visit a few years ago and found that when Haskins got out of jail,
he took over our old homeplace and built a fine house where our dogtrot
had been, and a pigpen over Ma's and Pa's graves. He can't bring himself
to tell Josie or Patrick or William, and I never will neither. The only
good part is that Haskins is dead now—died of some kind of cancer, and
real painful, I hear.

The wind simmers down as the sun starts setting into a cold grey
cloudbank in the west. So does my daydream of days gone by, which
could go on and on if I had the time to let it—there's plenty left to tell
where this story lets off, and, Lord willin', plenty more to come. There
ain't much left in my life to remind me of those days, except memories
blown back to me on the cold north wind ... and a little leather pouch,
worn smooth and shiny over the years, that I keep hidden in the back of
my bureau drawer. Only the spirit of the chief who gave it to me knows
what's in it; all I know is, on the whole, it's been mighty good medicine
for "Rockhand" Lizzie.

Reckon I might try to fetch in those cuptowels now before it rains,
and put some cornbread in the oven. I worry about Mark out driving at
his age, but it ain't that far to town, and I wouldn't deny him the little
pleasure of his afternoon domino game at the store with his friends.

Too bad he never got the hang of pitching worshers.

I might even have let him win once in awhile.

ABOUT THE AUTHOR

GERALD EUGENE NATHAN STONE was born in the South Canadian River bottoms in Oklahoma, and grew up in Arkansas, where he graduated from the University of Arkansas with degrees in Fine Arts and Architecture. After receiving a Divinity degree from Southwestern Baptist Theological Seminary, he served as pastor of churches in Knoxville and Little Rock. He returned to architecture, practicing in Denton, Texas, for thirty years. With his wife, Virginia, he left for California to "see the elephant," to spend time writing this book and to begin another. They presently live in Pacifica, California.

ALSO BY GERALD EUGENE NATHAN STONE:

GOD'S FRONT PORCH